"Hot chocolat[e] [...] sounding holl[ow]"

Ryder attempted a[...] was an alarming sha[de of white.]

"Or something stronger?" Annabeth asked, nodding at the test on the bathroom sink. There was no mistaking the bright blue plus mark in the test window. "Definitely something stronger."

He was staring at her, his blue eyes so piercing it was hard not to cringe away. But she didn't. She met his gaze, refusing to buckle or fall apart. When he pulled her into his arms, she couldn't decide whether to brush him off or melt into him.

"It's late." Ryder's voice was soft, his arms slipping from her. "You... I... I should let you get some sleep." He glanced at the test. "I better go."

Keep it together, Annabeth. This is best. At least she knew what to expect. The biggest surprise was how devastated she felt when he pulled the front door closed behind him, leaving her with two steaming mugs of cocoa and one bright blue pregnancy test.

Dear Reader,

Welcome back to Stonewall Crossing!

If you read *A Cowboy's Christmas Reunion*, you know that Stonewall Crossing is a small town built on tradition and full of lively characters. I grew up in places like this. With corner stores and soda fountains, beauty salons and town-wide holiday celebrations. Where Friday nights meant packed high school football games or rodeo arenas. In a place like this, no one is a stranger for long—and no one has secrets.

Ryder Boone is the black sheep of the Boone family. He was a lot of fun to write—inspired by one of my all-time favorite bad boys: Dean Winchester from *Supernatural*. He loves cars and women. His devotion to his family is unwavering even if "it's complicated." And let me tell you, things get all kinds of complicated for Ryder.

Annabeth Upton is a widow, mother to a young son and the principal of Stonewall Crossing Elementary School. Life hasn't been easy on her, but she finds a way to take things in stride and make lemonade out of even the bitterest lemons. But scandal in a small town isn't easy to survive, and she's facing the worst kind of scandal. Unless she can learn to trust her heart.

I love exploring the dynamics in a large family. In my experience, nobody is normal or perfect. But that's part of being a real family, working through hard situations, finding the humor in things and holding on to one another. Ryder and Annabeth have a lot to learn in this book.

I hope you enjoy visiting Stonewall Crossing, and I look forward to seeing you again real soon!

Happy reading!

Sasha

TWINS FOR THE REBEL COWBOY

SASHA SUMMERS

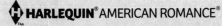

Recycling programs
for this product may
not exist in your area.

ISBN-13: 978-0-373-75604-9

Twins for the Rebel Cowboy

Printed in U.S.A.

Sasha Summers is part gypsy. Her passions have always been storytelling, romance and travel. Whether it's an easy-on-the-eyes cowboy or a hero of mythic proportions, Sasha falls a little in love with each and every one of her heroes. She frequently gets lost with her characters in the world she creates, forgetting those everyday tasks like laundry and dishes. Luckily, her four brilliant children and her hero-inspiring hubby are super understanding and helpful.

Books by Sasha Summers

Harlequin American Romance

The Boones of Texas

A Cowboy's Christmas Reunion

To the lovers of bad boys and
those hoping to reform them.

Writing is hard work. But I have an amazing team!
I am so thankful for my brainstorming (and "focus")
team: Allison, Marilyn, Patricia, Joni, Storm and
Jolene. To the best agent, Pam Hopkins, and my
wonderful editor, Johanna Raisanen, who make my
books better. To cowboys, for your infinite
hero inspiration. And for the love and support
of my wonderful, funny and inspiring kids!

Chapter One

If she'd been told she'd be spending the evening stranded in a honky-tonk bar, karaoke-ing her heart out to a room-ful of truckers, Annabeth Upton would have laughed. She didn't go to bars and she'd never been a fan of karaoke. But today had been tough. Tough as in her job was on the line, the phone creditors were getting nasty and her car slid across an icy road into a ditch. *Tough* might be an un-derstatement.

In the past three hours, she'd played a few rounds of dominoes and won a game of pool while waiting for news on her car. And since she had no way home and the storm outside was still pelting the tin roof with hail and sleet, the only options left were karaoke or getting drunk. She wasn't a big fan of hard liquor, so she'd start with karaoke. After that, and her day from hell, she might need a drink.

Thankfully, her audience wasn't too picky. People started calling out requests when she finished the first song. Four songs later, she was ready to pass the micro-phone. But since Etta James's "At Last" was one of her all-time favorite songs, she wasn't about to say no to the old guy who requested it. "Last one, for you," she said.

She cleared her throat, spun the microphone in her hand and waited for the music to play.

She could worry about the car and the repair bill later.

And the courtesy call from the school board informing her that the job she was temporarily filling was opening for interviews. Hopefully she'd proved herself during her emergency appointment. Hopefully the whole interview and vetting process was a formality, not something to give her ulcers. She'd wanted to be principal of Stonewall Crossing Elementary since she was a little girl and she couldn't imagine giving it up. Or how they'd make it if she had to go back to a teacher's salary. Not that there was a thing she could do about that right this second.

Grandma Flo would tell her worrying would get her wrinkles, a bad taste in her mouth and not much else. She took a deep breath.

"At last—" her voice rasped out, steady and on-key. So far so good. She closed her eyes and let the music carry her.

She kept singing, her nerves easing. She should be grateful. Her accident hadn't been too bad, and Cody was safe with her in-laws instead of with her. If he'd been in the car when she'd slid into the ditch… Nope, not going there. He was safe and sound and, other than the car, she'd walked away with only a bump on the head.

Her voice grew raw and thick as she continued.

Someone whistled, making her smile.

She fumbled the words as the door opened, blowing in cold air and sheets of ice before it slammed shut. A few people yelled, irritated by her singing or the interruption, she didn't know which.

She sucked in a deep breath, hoping for a big finish. She held the last note, soaking up the applause from the inhabitants of Ol' Ned's BBQ & Bar. She held her long crushed-velvet skirt in her hands, crossed her boot-clad ankles and curtseyed. Then she headed straight for the bar.

Ol' Ned was a mountain of a man, covered in a mask of long, thick facial hair. Other than his full lips—which were curved into a smile—he was fairly indistinguish-able. He slid a shot glass across the bar to her. "That one's from Mikey here." Ned nodded at the older man sitting to her left.

She stared at the amber-colored liquid. Why not? She winced, swallowing the liquid before she could second-guess herself. It burned all the way down her throat. "Thank you," she croaked to Mikey.

Mikey laughed.

"And the other's on the house," Ned rumbled, sliding another shot her way. "Voice like an angel."

"Ain't that the truth?" Mikey agreed.

She smiled, flattered in spite of herself. Her all-state choir days were long behind her, but she still loved to sing.

"Looks like one, too," Mikey added.

Ned spoke up. "She's too young and too pretty for you, Mikey."

"Ah, Ned, come on now." Mikey laughed. "A man's never too old to appreciate a fine-looking woman. Besides, the missus would skin me alive if I tried to trade her in for a younger model."

Annabeth's smile grew. "I'll try to remember you're spoken for." She saluted them both with her second shot and emptied the little glass, welcoming its warmth.

Mikey winked at her.

"Well, hell, darlin', I'm not spoken for." Another new voice had her spinning her stool around. This guy hadn't been here earlier, because she would have noticed him. For one thing, he was under fifty. For another, he was easy on the eyes. But he was staring at her as if she was a prize elk and he was a big-game hunter. "Play?" He held a pool cue out to her.

Yes, she could play. But this cocky guy hadn't been here earlier to know that. Greg had taught her to play. She was good—good enough to win a little money when she was in college. And right now, with two shots warming her belly, she was beginning to feel a little cocky herself. "Sure." She took the cue, ready to wipe the confidence off Mr. Ego's face.

"How about a bet?" he asked, stepping closer. "I'm feeling…lucky."

You need *a breath mint.* She glanced at the floor, trying not to giggle. She was going to teach this joker a lesson, and enjoy it. "That's nice." She arched an eyebrow. "You'll need it."

Mr. Ego laughed, invading her personal space. "And the bet?"

She put her hand on her hip, thinking. "I win, you sing a song." She winked at Ned, her tequila-infused courage goading her on.

"What do I get if I win?" he asked, looking at her boobs.

She poked his chest with her pool cue. "Eyes up here, buddy."

"Troy," he said. "I'm guessing your name is Angel?"

Oh, please. "No. Well, Troy, what were you hoping to get? And we'll go from there."

Troy winked. "Your number."

She bit her lip to keep from laughing. Apparently tequila made her giggly. He was not getting her number. She glanced at Ned and Mikey. Ned's arms were crossed, his eyebrows dipped so low she couldn't make out any evidence of his eyes. Mikey was leaning back against the bar, sizing Troy up. So they weren't Troy fans, either.

"Try again." She smiled sweetly at Troy.

Troy shook his head. "A drink?"

That seemed harmless enough. After all, Ned and Mikey were keeping an eye on things. She was going to beat him, anyway. "Sure."

He held out his hand, his smile a little unnerving. "Shake on it."

She put her hand in his, a flick of unease racing down her spine.

"Annabeth?" That was a voice she recognized.

Ryder Boone, all intense and broody, was making his way to her side. She sighed, relieved to have someone familiar show up. But Ryder was staring at Troy, eyes narrowed and assessing. Ryder stepped between her and Troy, putting her eye level with his wall of a chest, and cupped her face in his rough hands. She frowned at Ryder, startled by his touch. Was something wrong? "Ryder, what are you—?"

And then he kissed her. Ryder was kissing her. Ryder Boone was kissing her?

Not just any nice-to-see-you peck, either. His lips always looked full, soft and inviting. Now she knew they felt that way, too. They were like heaven, nipping at her lower lip until she was gasping. She swayed into him, the steel of his arms catching her and pulling her closer. Her head was spinning, too mixed-up to process what she was feeling... Only one thing was absolutely certain—Ryder Boone could kiss. It might have been almost six years since a man's kiss had every inch of her aching with want, but Ryder had her aching and wanting, desperately. Now.

His lips parted hers, the tip of his tongue touching hers. Her fingers dug into his leather jacket, clinging. His mouth lifted from hers, the rough pad of his thumb brushing across her lower lip.

Ryder. She was all hot and bothered. Over Ryder.

"Ready to go, Princess?" Ryder's voice was gruff.

She shook her head, trying to shake the fog of desire from her brain. Why wasn't he kissing her anymore? Wait. What the hell was happening?

"Princess?" he repeated.

Right, he was asking her something. "'Go'?" she managed, staring up at Ryder. Was he serious? And if he was, did he mean what she thought he meant? They may have flirted for years, years and years, but he'd never touched her. Besides, it would have been weird, since he was Greg's best friend.

"She's not going anywhere." Troy spoke up. "We just made a bet, didn't we, Annabeth?" Troy might be grinning, but he wasn't happy. The change in his stance was subtle but clear. Troy was bracing for a fight.

And Ryder was ready. His sky-blue gaze fixed on Troy, the slightest tick in his jaw muscle revealing his agitation. She shivered, stepping closer to Ryder warily.

Ryder's hands rubbed her arms, his attention returning to her. He arched an eyebrow, smiling his I'm-going-to-rock-your-world-tonight smile at her. She'd seen it in action, many times. Not that she'd ever been on the receiving end of it…before. Was he serious? Or was she having a reaction to the tequila?

"What's it gonna be, Princess?" His lips brushed her brow while his fingers threaded through hers. "You want to finish your game? Or you ready to go?"

His scent filled her nostrils, further clouding her mind. She blinked, the slightest tremble running down her spine. "Now?"

He bounced his eyebrows playfully, his gaze focused on her mouth. "Now."

And then he kissed her again. It wasn't a soft, slow sort of kiss, either. He twisted her hair through his fingers, tugging her head back as his mouth devoured hers. She went from light-headed to holding on for dear life. His breath, his tongue, his soft little growl as he deepened the kiss. She was drowning and she loved it.

He broke off slowly, breathing hard. He seemed just as stunned as she was. Could he want her the way she was wanting him? "Ready?" His voice was gruff.

She managed a nod. She was ready. Until this second, she hadn't realized just how ready she was. And never in a million years had she expected to do *this* with Ryder. But now, yes please, she was ready.

"Night, boys." Ryder touched the brim of his cowboy hat in mock salute, threw some cash on the bar, slid his arm around her waist and led her to the door.

It was frigid outside, but all she felt was the slow burn in her belly and the startling heat of Ryder's palm against her side. By the time he'd loaded her into his truck and climbed up beside her, Annabeth was buzzing with anticipation. She didn't think about why he'd decided tonight was the night or what might happen tomorrow. Nope, she climbed into his lap, knocked his black felt hat into the backseat, cradled his face between her hands and kissed him. It had been so long…so damn long. And she was lonely.

Ryder was Ryder. She'd never thought about having a hot one-night stand but, if she was going to, Ryder was probably the best candidate. He knew what he was doing, according to his conquests, and he didn't want complications.

"Princess," he growled.

"Shh," she answered, sliding her hands under his shirt to feel the rock-hard abs beneath. She shivered, frantically sliding his belt free and unbuttoning his pants. "I need this, Ryder. I need you."

RYDER HAD TO stop this.

Seeing Annabeth with Troy Clark, knowing the way Clark operated, had goaded him into action. He was running on a couple hours of sleep, so he wasn't in the best condition for a fight. Kissing Annabeth seemed…easier. Clark was an ass, but he'd back off if he thought Annabeth was with Ryder. Ryder never guessed she'd react this way—that *he'd* react this way.

This was Annabeth. The Annabeth who'd defended him from bullies in first grade. The Annabeth who'd helped him with hours of English homework. The Annabeth he'd taught to drive stick. The Annabeth who'd married his best friend. She was Greg's widow—off-limits, the "princess." She was a good girl, too good for him—and always would be. He had no right to touch her.

But she said she needed this, needed him.

And, damn him, he'd always wanted her.

Her hands slipped into his hair, tugging frantically. He groaned, pressing her to him, savoring the feel of her. One hand slipped beneath her sweater, greedily cupping her full breast. The weight of it in his palm made him moan. She shook, a broken little sob spilling into the cold air. It was his kiss she craved, grasping the back of his neck and pulling him closer. And his touch that made her breathing hitch and her entire body tremble. He watched, letting her move against him. She was lost, pulling his hair, eyes closed, her long neck arched back as she came apart on his lap.

His heart was pounding. She was the most beautiful thing he'd ever seen. Hair a mess, lips swollen. His fingers traced the seam of her mouth as she sighed, her arms wrapping around his neck. He couldn't wait. His hands were relentless—stroking, touching, pushing her long skirt past her thighs to her waist. With one tug, her underwear ripped free. Nothing separated them. And he couldn't wait. She was warm, encasing him deep inside her. Her ragged whisper of "Oh Ryder" drove him on.

His hands slid up her back, the silk of her skin and the brush of her soft curves inflaming him. He smoothed her hair back, his hands exploring her body, her curves, her softness. His nose brushed along the length of her neck, inhaling her scent. His lips latched on to her earlobe, making her gasp. Her hands moved up his chest, sliding along his shoulders to cradle his head. She arched against him, groaning hoarsely as they fit more deeply together. It was her groan that struck some sort of primal chord inside him. All at once, she was everywhere, holding him, overwhelming his senses. He gritted his teeth, fighting for control as she lost herself in the passion. Her body bowed, every inch of her tightening around him.

Her release sent him over the edge. His climax hit hard, rocking him from his boots to every hair on his head. He couldn't breathe, couldn't think… All he could do was hold on. He gripped her hips, desperate to keep her tight against him. Even when it was over, he couldn't ease his hold on her, couldn't let her go—he didn't want to. He wanted to etch the feel of her, the smell of her, into his mind before she slipped away. His hands tangled in her hair as he kissed her. He'd do whatever he could to hold on to this intimacy before the reality of what had happened sank in.

Annabeth ended the kiss, shaking her head. "Ryder…" she gasped, her voice unsteady.

How could he make this better? He smoothed her hair, but couldn't look at her. He didn't know what to do. But he knew he needed to do something.

"Ryder?" There was already regret in her voice, he heard it.

"Annabeth—" But that was all he managed to whisper. What could he say? He was banging his dead best friend's wife in the cab of his truck. His head fell back against the seat. He'd ruined everything—like he always did. "Shit," he murmured, still gasping for breath. As soon as the word slipped out, he knew he'd sent the situation from bad to worse.

She tried to climb off his lap but wavered, her skirts pinned beneath him. He caught her, cradling her close and breathing in her scent. He wasn't used to feeling uncertainty, or panic. But something about her pushing away from him, almost as if she couldn't bear his touch, filled him with bone-deep loss. He pulled her skirts free and let her go, watching her smooth her clothing into place. She sat stiffly at the end of the bench seat, looking just as dazed and confused as he felt.

He started the truck, adjusting his clothes as discreetly as possible. His mind worked overtime, looking for something to say to break the silence filling the cab of his truck.

"Why…were you here?" she asked, running her fingers through her long golden hair.

"Jasper called."

She glanced at him. "Who?"

"The mechanic here. One that towed your car in? He told me what kind of car had slid off the highway and I knew it had to be you…your car. Figured you'd need help… or be stranded." Greg's car. No one else drove a midnight-blue 1967 Impala in this part of Texas. Which meant Annabeth, maybe Cody, was involved. Greg's wife. Greg's family. He swallowed, clearing his throat. She didn't need to know the phone call had scared the shit out of him. He'd left all his lights on, and the door to his apartment was probably open. "I'll have to order parts for Lady Blue." Best thing about Greg's car, it was all metal. He didn't want to think about what might have happened to Annabeth if she'd been driving anything else. "Glad you're okay."

"Thank you." She was using her principal voice now, never a good sign.

"On your way to get Cody?" he asked. She didn't say

anything, so he risked a glance her way. She was staring out the window, nodding. So she wasn't going to talk to him. Fine. Why should he expect her to? He'd just taken advantage of her. In his truck cab. He shook his head, his hold tightening on the steering wheel.

What the hell was he thinking? Hadn't he screwed up enough relationships in his life? Annabeth wasn't just another woman, she was his friend. And he didn't have many of those.

He glanced at her, wishing he had the words to fix this. Instead, he got caught up in how damn pretty she was. Pretty and smart and funny. Good and innocent and sweet. He stared straight ahead, turning the windshield wipers up.

Annabeth Upton was the marrying type, not the one-night-stand type. He called her Princess to remind him of that. *Didn't work tonight.* He'd broken his promise to Greg and jeopardized one of the only friendships that mattered to him.

He hit ice several times, but he kicked his truck into 4x4 mode with no problems. It took twice as long to get back to Stonewall Crossing. By the time they turned into Annabeth's neighborhood, the ice had turned to snow.

He pulled into her driveway, leaving the truck running and the lights on. "Let me check the power." He held his hand out for her keys. All it took was a hard rain and half of the small town lost power. An ice storm could be downright crippling.

She put the keys in his hand, barely looking at him.

He slammed the truck door behind him and hurried up the first two steps of the porch, slipped and landed, hard, on his butt.

"You okay?" Her voice was laced with unmistakable laughter.

"Yeah, yeah," he answered, sliding as he managed to

stand. "Laugh it up, Princess." But, sore butt and all, he'd rather she was laughing than giving him the silent treatment.

He made sure the tiny house had electricity and the faucets were working before heading back to the front door.

Annabeth stood just inside. She looked at him, blushed and then hung her coat on one of the pegs behind the door. "Sorry you had to go out in that."

"Nothing else to do," he shrugged. Which was a piss-poor thing to say. He'd gone because it was her—period.

She rolled her eyes. She'd been rolling her eyes since he could remember. It always made him smile.

"Good damn thing, too, or you'd have ended up alone at Ned's place." His shoved his hands into his pockets. "Troy Clark is bad news, Annabeth."

She crossed her arms over her chest. "Really?"

"Yes, really," he snapped. "You don't know what kinda guy he is."

"Maybe. But I didn't end up with my skirts around my ears in his truck tonight, did I?" She flopped into a chair, covering her face in her hands. "I can't believe…" She shook her head. "I… I…"

He stared at her then, murmuring, "I'm sorry." It wasn't enough. His good intentions didn't matter. He hadn't stopped things from getting carried away. Instead, he'd held on to her for dear life, wanting her so bad it hurt. What was worse, he knew he'd do it again if he could. Only this time he'd love her the way she should be loved, take his time, in bed, and worship every inch of her.

"Ryder?" She looked up at him. Her huge hazel eyes sparkled with unshed tears.

If she cried, he'd be useless. He knew what needed to happen next. "It was sex, Annabeth, that's all." Damn fine sex, in his mind. "Best if we pretend tonight didn't happen." No matter how hard that might be for him.

She sniffed, nodding.

But then an awful realization occurred to him. "You're on the pill, right?"

Annabeth went completely white, then red, her hands fisting in her lap. "No. No, I'm not. Because I'm a widow. A widow with a five-year-old. I haven't…since Greg died. So no."

It was Ryder's turn to sink into a chair. "Shit."

"You already said that once." She stood, paced into the kitchen, then back. "Why didn't you use something? I mean, you're *you*."

He shook his head. "I didn't think… I never thought we'd…" He broke off, words failing him. "It's *you*."

"What does that mean, it's me?" Her hands were on her hips. "You were all over me."

"I was trying to get you out of there—"

"For sex."

He shook his head.

"But…but you kissed me," she argued, a range of emotions crossing her face. She stopped pacing, to glare at him. "Wait, back up. You came to get me because Jasper called. Then you saw me with Troy and went all caveman? Is that what you're saying? You didn't want Troy to have me, but you didn't want me—" She broke off, red-faced and trembling.

He didn't say a thing. She was right. *Initially*, that was what had happened. He opened his mouth, took one look at her, and closed it again.

"So, I was this pathetic—" Her voice broke. "You were trying to stop some sleazy hook-up guy and I—I *forced* myself on you?"

"You didn't force anything." But now wasn't the time to tell her he'd always wanted her. "Annabeth—"

She held her hand up. "I really appreciate the ride home, Ryder, but I need you to go."

"Wait." He gripped her shoulders. "What if you are preg—"

"Do not finish that sentence." Annabeth glared up at him. "It's just…sex, right? Tonight didn't happen. You picked me up and brought me home. The end."

"Now, Annabeth—"

"That's it," she cut him off.

"Wait."

"No!" she yelled.

He stared at her, gritting his teeth. God, she was stubborn. And beautiful. And soft…and warm. His stomach tightened.

"Just go." Her voice was shaking. She was shaking.

Leaving didn't feel right.

"Please," she added. "Go."

"I'll go," he murmured, forcing himself to release her.

She nodded, watching him.

He pulled his coat closed, opened the door and stepped out.

A gust of cold air blasted him, carrying a faint cry of distress to him. He froze, turning in the direction of the sound and slipped. He landed flat on his back. "Shit!" he yelled, half on Annabeth's icy walkway and half in the icy-wet grass. He sighed, staring up at the sky.

He heard the noise again, a long, pitiful sound.

Annabeth's voice rang out, "Oh my God! Are you okay?"

"I'm fine. Stay there."

"Ryder—" She burst out laughing.

He heard the sound again, a long, pitiful wail. He pushed himself up into a sitting position. "You hear that?"

But she was laughing too hard to hear him.

He shook his head, pushing himself onto his feet. He stood, listening. The sound started again, then another. From the house behind Annabeth's. "That house still vacant?"

"The Czinkovic place? Sadly, yes." She wrapped her arms around her shoulders. "Why?"

"You don't hear that?" he asked. "Now that you're done laughing?"

She grinned, but didn't say anything. They stood still, listening to the roar and whistle of the wind, and the faint cry coming from the empty house. "What is it?" she asked, stepping carefully onto the front porch.

"I'll find out," he said.

Chapter Two

Annabeth watched her sweet little boy's eyes go round as her grandmother chattered away.

"And then I found my teeth in my underwear drawer." Grandma Florence patted Cody on the head.

Cody put the escaping gray kitten—the kitten making such a terrible racket the night of the storm—back on Grandma Florence's lap. "Oh."

Annabeth shook her head, stirring the onions in the skillet. "Grandma, I can get you another case for your dentures." At least her grandmother only lost the storage containers and not the dentures themselves. That would get expensive real quick.

"It won't do any good." Her grandmother leaned forward, her whisper low and conspiratorial. "Because they're not *lost*. Someone's taking them. I think it's that Franklyn. He's always in my things, digging around. And he has that look."

Annabeth knew the medical assistants at Grandma Florence's home didn't get much pay or much thanks, but poor Franklyn didn't have a thieving bone in his body. What he did have was the patience of a saint. "What look?" Annabeth glanced at the older woman.

"You know…that look." Florence screwed up her face

in horror. "Like he's watching me. Plotting things. Up to no good."

Cody burst out laughing at his great-grandmother's expression, making it impossible for Annabeth not to laugh, too.

The tiny prick of needlelike claws drew Annabeth's attention down to her calves. Tom was hanging from her jeans, his little white-tipped tail sticking straight up. He mewed, his pink tongue on full display.

"You're adorable," Annabeth said to the kitten. "But it's a good thing I don't have a spatula in my hands or—"

"Ma," Cody reprimanded her, kneeling at her feet to gently detach Tom from her pant leg. "Be good." Cody lifted the kitten in his arms, carefully cradling the animal as he carried it across the room to the box he'd made for its bed.

"Cats in the kitchen." Grandma Florence clicked her tongue. "Never heard of such a thing. Cats are barn critters. 'Course one time we had a cat that got too close to the—"

"Grandma Flo." Annabeth was quick to interrupt. Her grandmother was rarely lucid enough to have a real conversation, but the old woman had a never-ending stream of stories to share. And not all of them had child-friendly endings. "How's work?"

Florence sighed. "I've never met such a lazy group of people in my life, Hannah."

Annabeth turned back to the cooking with a smile. Grandma Florence had dementia. On good days, Florence would call her Annabeth. But sometimes Annabeth was Hannah, Florence's daughter and Annabeth's mom, or Glenna, Florence's sister.

"You do the best you can," Annabeth encouraged her.

"I do." Her grandmother nodded. "I do. Someone's got to run a tight ship."

Grandma Florence ran the assisted-living community where she lived. At least that's what Grandma Florence thought. And the staff cooperated, within reason, to keep the feisty old woman under control. So far, it was the only facility Grandma Florence hadn't successfully escaped. Annabeth hoped it would stay that way, or they'd have to move her again—and the next facility was two towns over.

Cody giggled, making Annabeth glance his way. He lay with the kitten on his chest. Tom seemed just as delighted, nuzzling and licking Cody's nose.

The sheer joy in his laughter warmed her heart. God knew she didn't want or need something or someone else to look after. Managing Cody, work and her grandmother didn't leave her time for herself—let alone a stray fur ball. But Ryder had worked for a half hour to free the little guy from the abandoned house next door, and she couldn't turn it out into the freezing cold.

Cody's giggle jerked her back to the present. He pulled a colorful string of yarn across the floor, and Tom scampered after it, all ears and tail and gray fluff. Her sweet boy never asked for anything, so how could she tell him no when he'd asked to keep Tom? She didn't. And now Cody and Tom were inseparable—unless Tom was climbing up her pants, panty hose, the curtains or the tablecloth.

There was a knock on the door. "Anyone home?" Ryder called out.

Ryder… She'd spent four weeks refusing to think about that night. Or Ryder. Or how mortified she was. She never acted without thinking things through. She could blame either the two shots or Ryder's kiss for her outrageous behavior. She hoped, for everyone's sake, it was the shots.

She took a deep breath before calling out her standard "Nope." Sure, he hadn't dropped by for dinner since *it* happened, but he used to. All the time. If she was being completely honest with herself, she—and Cody—had missed him. And there was no point in getting weird about things, either. Ryder was a part of her life. She liked having him around.

She'd just have to try harder to forget every touch, scent and sound from that night…or the way she ached when she thought about his hands on her. So she just wouldn't think about it.

"You sure?" Ryder called out.

"R-r-ryder," Cody laughed. "Mom's m-making 'sgetti."

"With meatballs? Smells good," Ryder said. Annabeth turned as he walked into her small yellow kitchen, heading straight for Florence. "Well, if it isn't the prettiest gal I know."

Florence waved him to her wheelchair. "Get yourself on over here and give me a kiss."

"Try to stop me," Ryder said, hugging the older woman's frail body tightly and kissing her cheek.

"I was wondering when you were coming home, Michael. It's not good to spend so much time at the office. Especially when you've got a pretty little wife like Hannah, here, waiting at home." She patted Ryder's hand. "You're a lucky man. You need to treat her right."

Ryder looked at Annabeth. "Don't I know it."

Annabeth rolled her eyes, wishing his teasing didn't sting. He might have chosen to be alone, but she hadn't. Life was work, work she'd always thought she'd share with someone. She wanted to treasure the same memories, the same people, with someone who knew and loved her soul. But Greg was gone. Dating wasn't on her detailed master plan for the next five years or so.

"Cody," she spoke to her son. "Wash up and come to the table, please."

"Yes, Ma." Cody put the kitten in its padded box bed.

"Stay put," he whispered, rubbing its little head before he hurried down the hall to the bathroom.

"Cats in the kitchen," Grandma Florence said. "Never heard of such a thing." Ryder steered her wheelchair to the table.

"You staying for dinner?" Annabeth asked him as she set another place. At this distance it was hard to miss the bandage around his wrist and the dark, greenish-yellow smudge on his brow. "What happened?" She didn't know which was worse: fighting or bull riding. She wasn't a fan of either, but Ryder was Ryder.

"Bull wanted me to get better acquainted with the wall of the arena. So I obliged and flew straight into the pipes." He held up his wrist. "Just a sprain. Almost healed up now." Ryder cocked an eyebrow, his crooked smile doing a number on her. "Don't you worry your pretty little head over me."

She sighed, loudly. He laughed.

"Did it h-hurt?" Cody asked, staring at his wrist.

"Nah." Ryder shook his head. "After breaking my collarbone, this was nothing."

She remembered visiting him in the hospital then. "You were in so much pain."

"Your lemon bars helped," he answered, with a wink.

"I imagine the pain meds did, too." She shook her head.

"Ma's l-lem-mon bars are great," Cody agreed.

"Totally." Ryder nodded, sitting at the table. "And, since you're asking so nicely, I'd love to stay for dinner."

"Ma," Cody sat. "Can I take T-T-Tom for show-and-tell?"

"Tom, huh?" Ryder asked, serving Florence some spaghetti.

Cody nodded, watching Ryder.

"Good name." Ryder nodded at the boy.

And, just like that, her son was grinning from ear to

ear. She loved to see him smile like that, as if he was a carefree five-year-old. "We can't take animals to school, baby." She grinned at him, cutting up Grandma Florence's spaghetti. "But you can take in a few pictures if you want."

Cody nodded. "'Kay."

"Lady Blue's ready. Parts came earlier this week," Ryder said around a mouthful of spaghetti. "She's purring like a kitten—" He winked at Cody. "Good as new."

"Great." She poked at the pasta on her plate. If Lady Blue was ready, then so was the bill. She still had almost twenty thousand to pay off on Grandma Florence's last hospital stay. But she'd figure something out. She always did. "Guess it's a little harder to work with an injured hand?"

"Not really. I'm good with both my hands." His words made her warm all over.

"How's Mags, Teddy?" Grandma Florence asked Ryder. Teddy was Ryder's father, Mags his mom.

"She's fine, Flo." Ryder didn't miss a beat.

"You tell her I'm still waiting on her chicken pie recipe. That recipe…" Florence sighed and shook her head.

Dinner conversation flowed. Ryder had funny stories from his latest rodeo stint, how his cowboy hat had a hole "clean through it" after getting hooked by a bull. Somehow he managed to make his almost serious injury into a comedy. Cody could hardly wait to show Ryder the model car he was building. And Grandma Florence told them that there was a flasher running around the retirement home.

Sunday nights were her favorite. She didn't let herself think about the next day, the stress she was feeling—she tried not to.

She'd spent the past year being the principal Stonewall Crossing needed, and hopefully that was enough for the school board. But try as she might, she couldn't ignore that her assistant principal Ken Branson knew the right people, had money, *and* a wife and kids. He was the total package. And serious competition for the job—if he applied.

She realized Ryder was watching her and shrugged off her worries. Her worries would keep until the company was gone and Cody was in bed.

She stood, clearing the table while the others chattered on. When that was done, she pulled out the apple pie she and Cody had made earlier that day. The scent of cinnamon and sugar filled the air and soothed her nerves. She loved baking. She loved cooking. There was something about preparing a meal and feeding friends and family that made her happy.

She cut two decent pieces for Cody and Grandma Florence and a larger piece for Ryder.

He nodded at her when she put the plate in front of him, his blue eyes lingering on her face a little longer than normal.

"You got your momma's gift in the kitchen, Annabeth." Florence reached for Annabeth's hand.

Annabeth took it, kneeling by her chair to savor her grandmother's moments of clarity. "She said she learned everything from you."

Tears filled Florence's eyes. "'Course she did. It's a momma's job to train her daughter in the kitchen. What sort of a wife and mother would she be if she couldn't take care of her menfolk?" She winked at Ryder and smiled at Cody. "She'd be so proud of the woman you've become. Your daddy, too."

"I'm trying." Annabeth smiled.

"I know, Annabeth." Grandma Florence shook her head. "You work too hard sometimes."

"I do what needs to be done." Annabeth kissed her cheek.

Grandma Florence shook her head. "Who takes care of you?"

Annabeth couldn't answer that.

"Me," Cody piped up, kissing her on the cheek. "Right, Ma?"

Annabeth nodded, hugging him to her. "Yep."

"Lemme see that kitty o' yours, Cody." Grandma Florence patted Annabeth's hand. "Thank you for dinner, Annabeth. You never forget our Sunday dinner."

"It's something I look forward to every week, you know that." Annabeth held her grandmother's hand in both of hers. This woman had been the one to teach Annabeth what it was to be strong while keeping a sense of humor. There wasn't a day that went by that she didn't hear one of Grandma Flo's bits of wisdom in her head, guiding her.

"Here he is, Grandma," Cody announced. Tom was squirming in his arms but settled down once he was placed on Grandma Flo's lap.

"Well, he's a fine tomcat." Grandma Florence held the cat up, turning the mewling animal this way and that. "He'll have long legs. A good mouser."

"He will be fast." Cody babbled on, his stutter barely tripping him up he was so excited. And Grandma Florence, bless her, didn't say a thing.

Now if Annabeth could get the boys at school to stop teasing him, Cody might not be so quiet all the time.

RYDER PULLED THE dish towel off the hook by the sink. He smiled as he fingered the row of lemons stitched along the trim of the towel. No doubt Annabeth had stitched each one herself. Lemons were Annabeth's thing. She had a yellow kitchen with lemon-print curtains and lemon-print towels. Hell, she even smelled fresh and sweet like the fruit itself.

He swallowed, her scent tickling his nostrils as she leaned closer to place a dish on the rack.

"You don't have to," Annabeth murmured. "Rest your wrist."

He didn't say anything, just dried off the plates she'd stacked in the dish rack.

What would she say if he told her the injury was her fault? After he'd left the kitten in her hands, he'd spent the rest of the night drinking. He hadn't had more than a couple of hours' sleep when his riding and drinking buddy DB picked him up and took him to the rodeo. If he'd been thinking clearly, not torn up with guilt yet wanting her, it wouldn't have happened. He'd have been thinking about the ride, not her. Not that she'd see it that way. No, she'd argue with him, tell him he was a grown man capable of making his own decisions...

She sighed as he dried another dish. He smiled.

It was the least he could do after inviting himself to dinner. Annabeth always made something special for Florence's Sunday-night dinner. Annabeth always made him feel welcome. Florence and Cody made him feel wanted. Two things he never felt at his father's table. He'd stayed away the past few weeks and he'd missed it. But tonight, he had news he had to share.

All of his hard work, endless tinkering and attention to detail might just pay off. He was a master mechanic; engines just talked to him. And his bodywork was a work of art. Apparently, the owner of a big custom garage in Dallas agreed. According to his boss, John, Jerry Johannsson, known as JJ, had seen some of Ryder's bodywork and was impressed enough to track down Ryder's whereabouts. JJ had badgered John, who wasn't much of a talker, with all sorts of questions. Whatever John had said convinced JJ that Ryder should come for a visit. John wasn't happy about Ryder's interest, but he kept his opinions to himself. Maybe now Ryder would finally get out of Stonewall Crossing and away from his past.

As soon as John had told him, Ryder had headed to Annabeth's house to share the good news over dinner. If there was one person who would support him, it would be Annabeth.

But something was wrong, he could tell. Tension seemed to weigh Annabeth down, and he didn't like it. Whatever it was, his news could wait until he could fix whatever was wrong.

She tucked a long strand of her golden hair behind her ear, drawing his attention to her. To her ear…her neck. He spent plenty of time thinking about her—them—even though he knew better. Best thing he could do was find some sweet thing and wear himself out. Hell, the pretty medic that wrapped his wrist had offered to take him home for a more "thorough assessment." He'd been curious. Her cherry-kissed lips and fiery red hair were tempting. But in the end he'd gone home alone. Just like he had every night since the night he'd shared with Annabeth. And it scared the crap out of him.

"Dishwasher broken?" he asked.

She nodded. "I still remember how to operate a sponge, so we're good."

He grinned at her. "Bet I can fix it."

She shook her head.

"You don't believe me?" he teased, nudging her with his elbow.

She looked up at him, her hazel eyes so big he paused. "I know you can, Ryder. It's just…" She shook her head, plunging her hands back into the soapy water. "It's fine."

"Sure, if you like washing all your dishes by hand, maybe." He set the dish in the drying rack and waited.

She couldn't hold back her laugh, a free and easy sound. "Maybe I do."

"I know better, Princess." He took the plate she offered.

"Stop calling me that." She sighed. "You don't need to fix it. Okay? It's not a big deal."

"Right." He frowned. "It's a dishwasher."

She glanced at him, a tell-tale flush on her cheeks.

He sucked in a deep breath. "What?"

She shook her head, turning back to the dishes.

"What's eating you, Princess?" he murmured, willing her to look back at him.

"R-Ryder," Cody held up the kitten. "Tom saw Doc F-F-Fisher. Says Tom is a good cat."

"My brother would know. Fisher's all about cats and dogs." Ryder smiled at the boy and took the kitten, holding it up so they were eye to eye. The kitten swatted at Ryder's nose. "Plenty of energy." He laughed.

Cody nodded.

"That's an understatement," Annabeth added.

Ryder turned the kitten so it was nose to nose with her. The kitten started purring, his little paws kneading the air. She shook her head, but took the kitten and held it under her chin. "Yeah, yeah, you're adorable."

Ryder winked at Cody, who winked back. It was then that he noticed Grandma Florence snoring softly in her wheelchair.

"Naptime?" Ryder asked softly.

"She d-does that." Cody grinned. "Any new cars?" Cody loved talking about cars—he was a lot like Greg that way. Every now and then, he'd take Cody to John's garage with him. The boy had an endless fascination with the way things worked. He loved to tinker, putting things together, taking them apart. And Ryder respected that. A man should know how to work with his hands, to take care of things around the house and in the garage.

"Wh-what about the Cadillac?" Cody asked.

Ryder grinned. "Finished."

"Can I see it?" Cody asked.

Ryder looked at Annabeth in question.

"Not tonight," she hedged, not meeting his eyes. She handed Tom back to Cody, but Ryder saw the quick kiss she planted on the kitten's head. "I've got to get Grandma home and finish the laundry before bed. Then I have a little work to do."

He heard the exhaustion in her voice. "What can I do?" Ryder glanced at the clock.

She scowled. "Cody, go get your clothes picked out for tomorrow while I get Grandma's things together."

Ryder waited, knowing once Cody was out of the room he was going to get an earful.

"Ryder, you can't keep doing this." She pointed around the room. "People will talk."

"People? Like who?" he asked, resting his hip against the kitchen counter while she wiped down the stove top.

"People," she grumbled. "Like Lola Worley."

"Yeah, sure, Lola Worley probably is talking." He shrugged. Lola was one of three sweet blue-haired ladies who owned the only beauty shop on Main Street. She was courting the owner of the only bakery on Main Street, ensuring she'd hear all the gossip Stonewall Crossing had to offer. Lola had big ears and an even bigger mouth. But, according to some, she had an equally big heart. "What are they talking about?"

"Us," she snapped, clearly exasperated. "You. Being here *all* the time. Taking care of things."

"*All* the time?" He scratched his head. He hadn't been

here in a long time. Too long. She was worried about him being here? She'd never given a hoot before.

"Things are…different now." She swallowed.

He stiffened. Damn it all. "Why?" But he knew why.

"Because *this* is a big deal." She took the towel from him and hung it up.

His attention wandered to her mouth. So she had been thinking about what had happened between them? He wasn't the only one losing sleep over that night—

"The interim appointment is up in two months. The school board has already opened the principal position to applicants." Disappointment hit him hard, but he shoved it aside to listen to her. That was news to him. It explained the tension. She worked hard, harder than anyone he knew. She turned away, pacing the floor. "They have to, I know that, but I need this job." She sighed. "I'm sure Ken Branson will apply, and he knows everyone."

"Branson is a tool." Ryder snorted, trying to ease her mind. He'd never seen her this worked up. He placed his hands on her shoulders, aching to pull her close. "Annabeth, you'll get it." He smiled. "I've never known anyone as stubborn and persuasive as you, Princess. And that says a lot, coming from the family I do."

She smiled, relaxing a little.

"It's just, you're single and I'm single…" She shrugged.

"Good thing Grandma Flo's here to chaperone us," he teased, but knew there was more. "What else is going on?"

She shook her head, but her gaze wandered down the hallway to Cody's room.

"Cody?" he encouraged.

Her lips tightened, as though she was reining in her temper.

"He okay?" he spoke softly.

"The boys, at school," she whispered. "They're giving him a hard time about his stutter."

His anger was hot and fast, but he suspected she didn't need that right now. "Kids are mean, Princess, you know that. And Cody is tougher than you think." His hands tightened on her shoulders. "Who is it?"

She shook her head. "Nope." Her smile warmed him through.

He grinned. She knew him. "What?"

"The last thing I need is you threatening some school-kids." She rolled her eyes.

"Kids, no." He shook his head. "Parents, maybe."

She giggled. And he loved the sparkle in her eyes as her gaze connected with his. "Ryder—"

"Joking, Princess." He laughed. "Not that it's not tempting."

She nodded. "Yes. Very." Her expression shifted then, from amused to intense. Her gaze fixed on his, carefully searching. "You don't owe us anything, you know?"

His hands fisted. "Don't start that again, Annabeth—"

"Stop, Ryder." Her smile grew tight. "Greg wouldn't expect you to babysit Cody and me. Stop doing what you think he wants you to do."

Yes, he'd promised Greg he'd look out for them, but... How could he explain that he did it because he needed to? Taking care of them made him feel better, too, as though he was important to someone. "That's not why I do it."

Her forehead creased slightly. "It's not?"

"Time for checkers before I go." Grandma Florence sat up, her sudden declaration sending the kitten scurrying across the kitchen and into his box.

He smiled as Cody's squeal of delight came from his bedroom. "Think Cody heard you, Flo."

Two seconds later Cody came barreling into the kitchen

with his checkers box. "Ryder, you can play the w-w-win-ner," Cody said.

"Deal," he agreed, squatting in front of the dishwasher. "Gives me time to see what we need to fix this thing."

"Ryder," Annabeth started to argue.

He opened the dishwasher and peered inside. "Got a flashlight, Princess?"

"Ryder," she tried again, her tone sharper.

He smiled. "It's a little dark in here." He held his hand out.

"Here." Cody gave him a flashlight.

"Thanks, champ." Ryder clicked on the flashlight, inspecting the motor in the base of the near-ancient dishwasher. "It's the least I can do to pay you back for dinner." He heard her little grunt of frustration and grinned. "Why don't you go put your feet up for a second, relax." He could be just as stubborn as she was. And if she wouldn't tell him what was eating her, he'd take care of what he could.

Chapter Three

"You don't seem to understand how important this is." Winnie Michaels dabbed at the mascara running down her cheeks. "They're fifth graders, for Pete's sake. And it's one lil' bitty ol' point, Annabeth."

Annabeth kept her I'm-listening expression firmly in place. The principal before her, Davis Hamburg, had told her it was important to convey sincere empathy while never losing control of the situation. She'd been repeating this over and over for the past thirty minutes, but Annabeth and Winnie had been in the same class growing up and they hadn't exactly been pals. Annabeth had been one of the lucky recipients of Winnie Michaels's especially effective public shaming techniques. Winnie used to call her Annabeth Banana-breath and encouraged more than a few of her posse to chant along during gym class or recess. She received more than her fair share of banana bread, banana muffins, banana skins and browning bananas throughout her school years. It was ironic that the one thing Annabeth had craved when she was pregnant was bananas.

"That's just it, Ms. Michaels. Kevin was two points from passing. He'd have to get his grade up to audition for a solo in the spring concert," Mrs. Schulze, the music teacher, calmly explained.

But Annabeth didn't say a thing. Kevin Michaels was

a pain in her rear on a daily basis. He lied, cheated and picked on the younger kids—Cody among them. But when push came to shove, none of the kids would turn him in. Out of fear, she suspected, and there was nothing she could do about it. Kevin was just like his mom.

Winnie stared at her.

Annabeth stared back.

"I never thought you were the spiteful type," Winnie spoke softly. "That you'd punish my son for our childhood rivalry."

Mrs. Schulze looked acutely uncomfortable, glancing back and forth between the two of them expectantly.

Annabeth's eye twitched. "Once Kevin gets his grade up—"

"He'll be in middle school." Winnie shook her head, opening her cavernous purse and digging around inside it. "This is his last concert here." She pulled out a pair of gloves, three tubes of lipstick, a scarf, two phone chargers and a bag of what appeared to be pulverized goldfish crackers.

"He'll still perform in the chorus, Ms. Michaels," Mrs. Schulze tried again.

"With all the *little* kids." Winnie sighed. "It's *embarrassing.*"

"There are only four solo parts, Winnie," Annabeth spoke calmly. "Over thirty kids signed up to audition for the solos." She glanced at Mrs. Schulze, who nodded. "All of the other students will be in the chorus, that's most of fourth and fifth grade. Even if Kevin's grades were passing, there would be no guarantee he'd get a solo."

Winnie pulled out a wadded-up handkerchief and blew her nose. "Well, I think this is unfair, that's all there is to it."

"I'm sorry you feel that way," Annabeth continued.

"Did Kevin turn in the extra-credit assignments Mr. Glenn gave him?"

Winnie shrugged, shoving her things back into her purse. "You tell me, Annabeth. Since you know everything."

Annabeth resisted the urge to bury her head in her hands.

"This was a waste of my time, plain and simple. You don't like Kevin so you're singling him out. I don't know why we had this *meeting*," Winnie sighed.

Because Winnie had called and called and been so rude to the school secretary that Annabeth had given in. She knew it was useless. Parents signed a grade contract at the beginning of every year, they knew that only passing students were allowed to participate in extra-curricular activities—from field trips to school performances. Why Winnie thought Kevin was different was a mystery. But she'd keep her mouth shut and her *concerned* expression in place until she was alone in her office.

"I know people on the school board—" Winnie started in.

"I encourage you to bring your concerns to them, Winnie," Annabeth interrupted, stealing the other woman's threat. "If you feel the grade contract is unfair, the school board should review the policy."

Winnie pushed herself to her feet, scowling at Annabeth, then Mrs. Schulze. "I will. I will tell them my *concerns*. About you. And the way you're running this school." And with that Winnie Michaels stormed from her office.

"Can I get you anything, Ms. Upton?" Mrs. Schulze asked. "You look a little green around the gills."

Annabeth smiled. "I'm not a fan of confrontation."

"Well, you handled it like a pro. I'm sorry Kevin isn't up for a solo—" Mrs. Schulze broke off, crossing her arms over her chest. "Actually, I'm not. I'm not the least bit torn up about it."

Annabeth allowed herself a small grin. "It sounds like you have plenty of kids to audition. I'm sure you'll pick the best for the parts."

Mrs. Schulze nodded. "You go on home and get some rest. Don't let this hiring nonsense get to you. Everyone at the school knows you're the one for the job."

"Thank you, that means a lot." Annabeth shrugged. "Let's hope the school board agrees."

Mrs. Schulze paused in the doorway. "Cody does really well singing. Not one stutter. And he has a lovely voice. Just like his mama."

Annabeth grinned after the retreating teacher. She was lucky to have such a supportive staff.

"Sorry." Ken poked his head in. "Did I miss the meeting?"

"Yes." She stood, putting away two of the student files she'd pulled earlier in the day.

"How did Winnie take it?" he asked, leaning against the door.

Annabeth rested her hip against the desk. "She wasn't pleased." Which was why he'd missed the meeting. No one wanted to get on Winnie's bad side. But that was part of the job, following the protocol and enforcing the procedures in place—even if it meant an unhappy parent now and then. "But that's the necessity of the grade contract. Mr. Glenn tried to accommodate Kevin but he didn't do the extra credit."

Ken nodded.

She went back to straightening her desk, more than ready to leave for the weekend. "Anything else we need to talk about?" she asked nonchalantly.

"I'm interviewing for the position next week," he offered. "I know things could get awkward, but it's business, after all."

She looked at him, hoping she looked enthusiastic rather than nauseous. "Of course, Ken. I appreciate the heads-up. Good luck. I'm sure it will go well." She wished she could mean it, she really did. But it was the right thing to say.

He cocked an eyebrow at her. "I'm not a big believer in luck, Annabeth. It's all about working hard and fighting for what you want. And, to be frank, I want this position. But I hear I'm not the only one they're interviewing." He was watching her closely. "Besides you, it's me and two others. One from San Antonio and one from Illinois, with years of experience from what I hear." His laugh was forced. "Since that's something neither of us have, looks like a tough race is ahead."

Perfect. Just what she wanted to hear. Her phone rang.

"I'll let you get that." He pushed off the door frame. "Enjoy your weekend. Get some rest, you're looking worn-out."

"Night, Ken. You, too," she said before answering the phone. "Annabeth Upton," she snapped.

"Um… Hey, stranger," came Josie Boone's voice. "I was hoping to take you out to dinner tomorrow night. Sounds like you could use it."

"God, yes." Annabeth collapsed into her desk chair. "Just promise there will be wine."

"Tough week?" Josie asked.

"You could say that." She yawned. "I'm not sure I can get a sitter—"

"Bring him over to my dad's. He and Lola can play checkers or make cookies," Josie cut her off. "I just want to make sure you're okay."

"Why wouldn't I be?" She sighed, knowing she sounded defensive.

Josie laughed. "Well, you sound pretty wound up."

"Sorry," she groaned. "Guess I am." She powered down her computer. "I'll try to shake off the attitude before then, I promise. I'm picking up some fried chicken and watching a superhero movie with Cody tonight."

"A superhero movie, huh? Will there be a shirtless scene?"

"If I'm very lucky." She grinned. "Not all of us get to go home to a hunky husband."

"I am one lucky woman," Josie agreed. "So, tomorrow?"

"Sounds good. I'll call Lola first and make sure it's okay with her."

"Okay. Text me later. And enjoy your date with Cody."

Five minutes later she was collecting Cody from the gym. "Sorry I was a few minutes late, Cody."

"It's fine, Ma. Look." Cody started dribbling the basketball.

"Wow." She put her hands on her hips. "Look who's a dribbling pro."

"Coach taught me." Cody was still all smiles.

"Principal Upton?" A very fit, very handsome man approached. "Coach Goebel, just started. I'm subbing for Coach Hernandez while he's recovering from his back surgery."

She shook his hand. "Nice to meet you." Ken was in charge of all the substitutes, so meeting Coach Goebel was a surprise. Even more so because none of the teachers had mentioned him. Well, they might have. She'd been a little preoccupied with her upset stomach—and Winnie. But still, she could only imagine what the reaction to Coach Goebel had been. It wasn't every day a new, good-looking man came to town—married or not.

"You, too." He nodded. "Cody's a natural with a bas-ketball."

She ruffled Cody's hair. "His dad was, too."

"Does he still play?" Coach Goebel asked, watching Cody dribble in a wide circle.

"Who? Cody's dad?" Annabeth drew in a deep breath. "No, Greg was killed in Afghanistan about six years ago." It was getting easier to say. The ache was there, but the pain didn't bring her to her knees anymore.

"I'm sorry." He shook his head. "I lost a lot of buddies. Nice to be back and part of the world again. Don't miss it over there."

"You were military?" she asked.

"Army." He nodded. "Now, I'm a substitute coach. Single, carefree and loving every minute of it."

She heard the way he stressed *single* and looked at him. "Guess it's a pretty big change of pace?"

He smiled, the corners of his eyes crinkling nicely. "No complaints."

"Well, thanks for keeping Cody occupied while I closed up shop."

"It was fun." He shook his head. "Principal Upton—"

"Call me Annabeth."

"Bryan." He swallowed, clearly interested. "It was really nice talking to you, Annabeth."

Bryan Goebel was the last thing she needed. Besides the distraction he was likely to cause amongst her single and desperate staffers, he was a threat. All it would take was one look, one misconstrued conversation, and her already precarious employment situation would become ten times worse. God, Ken would have a field day... Her thoughts came to a screeching halt. "How did you hear about the position? Stonewall Crossing's a little off the beaten path."

"Ken." Bryan Goebel grinned. "We go way back. I was

thinking about a change of scenery. And he can be very persuasive."

Annabeth forced a smile. *I'll bet.* "Ken's always thinking." He was such an ass. "You ready, Cody?"

Cody nodded, dribbling the ball to the storage closet, and then running back to her side.

"You have a good weekend," Coach Goebel called after her.

"You, too, Coach," Cody answered.

Annabeth nodded in return, but her smile was forced. She'd like to think Ken was just helping out a former serviceman and friend. But she *knew* Ken. After all, he'd just said he'd fight for the job. And using a hot, single guy would definitely cause talk, if not serious problems, for her.

Right now, she had bigger things to worry about. She couldn't ignore it anymore, she had to get answers. She only hoped the answers were the ones she wanted.

RYDER KICKED THE blankets off and sat up. His phone was ringing. His pulse was racing ninety-to-nothing, his heart in his throat.

"Yeah?" he grumbled.

"Ryder?" It was Annabeth.

"What's wrong?" He rubbed a hand over his face, glancing at the alarm clock. It was midnight. "Everything okay?" Which was a stupid question. She wouldn't be calling if it was.

"No." She sounded strange, tense.

He froze, waiting for more information. "Annabeth?"

"Can you come over?" Her voice broke. "Now, please?"

He stood, pulling on his jeans. "On my way."

"Thanks," she murmured before hanging up.

He tucked the phone in his pocket, hurriedly tugging on a black T-shirt and leather jacket, and hopping into his boots as he headed out the door. He forced himself to take a few deep breaths, clearing his mind, before starting his motorcycle and heading toward Annabeth's place.

He wasn't a worrier by nature—he'd always sort of rolled with what life gave him. But the panic in Annabeth's voice had triggered an immediate response. She didn't scare easy. Or get rattled. Annabeth was solid, grounded…

She was home, not at the hospital—which meant she, Cody and Flo weren't injured or sick. Which was good. Still, she *had* called him, so there was something seriously wrong. He parked in her driveway. Her living room and kitchen windows were illuminated.

The door opened before he had time to knock. Annabeth stood just inside, pale, with red-rimmed eyes. He stepped inside, pushing the door closed behind him. "Hi."

She nodded, sniffing. "Can you…can you sit down? I need to talk…we need to talk."

"Everyone's okay?" he asked, adrenaline and anxiety coursing through his veins.

She had a hard time meeting his gaze. "Cody and Flo are fine." Her hazel eyes finally met his. "I'm sorry I woke you. And called you over…"

"It's fine." He rubbed her arms, his eyes searching hers. "All good."

She nodded, waiting for him to sit before she took a deep breath. "I know it's late… Actually I didn't realize how late it was." She frowned. "My mind wouldn't shut off. And I knew it couldn't wait. I mean, it could, but it couldn't—you know?"

No, he didn't know.

"Let me start by saying, I know you. I have no intention of attempting to change who you are." She was fidgeting, twisting her hands in front of her. "But what sort of person would I be if I didn't tell you?"

Ryder leaned forward, resting his elbows on his knees. What the hell was she talking about? "Annabeth—"

"I have two charts," she said, holding up one finger before hurrying into her small kitchen. She returned with two poster boards. Each had some sort of graph, with different color tabs and her clean script in the margins. "Option A or Option B. I've mapped out how much time we have, how we can handle this, who needs to be involved… I'm thinking the fewer the better."

Ryder glanced at the two boards, but it didn't clear anything up. "Annabeth—"

"Hold your questions," she interrupted. "Or I'll never get it all out."

He ran a hand over his face, sighed and sat back in the chair. Sure, why not? Not like he had someplace to be—like bed. Sleeping. "Shoot."

"Okay." She nodded, smiling tightly. "Okay. So, we're six weeks or so in. There's another couple of months before it goes public." She held up the two posters. "Option A is with you temporarily, Option B is without." She shrugged. "John mentioned something about a Dallas job when I picked up Lady Blue? Is that happening?"

He nodded, slowly answering, "It's a done deal."

"Well, congratulations." She scanned her posters, putting the Option A poster behind the couch. "I guess that's the question then. I'm sure you're excited to get out of Stonewall Crossing. I can do this on my own. No need to mess things up for you." She sat opposite him, gripping her poster.

"Princess," he murmured, smiling at her scowl. "I have no idea what you're talking about."

"Oh." She blinked, placing the poster facedown on her cluttered coffee table. "Ryder I… We are…" She sucked in a deep breath and shook her head.

He heard that strange nervous tension in her voice and moved to crouch in front of her. "Don't fall apart on me now."

"I won't." She sniffed. "I'm stronger than that."

"Don't I know it." He didn't resist the urge to smooth a strand of her long hair. The way she was looking at him… as if her world was falling apart and she needed rescuing… She wanted him here, but she still hadn't said why. This from a woman who was never short on words or opinions.

But she didn't say a thing. She just sat there, tense, quiet and pale.

He'd never wanted to hold someone as much as he wanted to hold her, right now. He said the first thing that came to mind. "Like the pajamas."

She ran her hands over her knees—clad in pale blue flannel pajamas, covered in rainbows and butterflies. "Cody got them for me last Christmas. Greg's folks took him shopping. They're my movie night pj's."

"What did you watch?" he asked, looking at the half-eaten bowl of popcorn and the empty juice box containers.

"*Superman.*" Her eyes were huge, boring into him with an intensity he felt deep in his bones. He ran his thumb along her temple, tucking a long strand of golden hair behind her ear. Touching her seemed to ground him, to ease the growing anxiety in his chest.

He smiled at her, earning a small smile in return. Ever since she'd tripped Tyler Gladwell on the playground and offered Ryder her hand, he'd known Annabeth was the kind of girl a fellow should hold on to forever. But Greg had beat him to it.

She blew out a shaky breath, her gaze slipping from his. It was easier for him to breathe then. Where had this pull come from? All he wanted was to touch her. Which was the last thing he should do. The last thing he had the right to do.

"So…" She stood, putting space between them.

"Why don't we start over?" he said, standing beside her. "I'm guessing you had a rough day?"

"Yes." She glanced at him, then swallowed.

"I can't fix it if I don't know what's wrong, Princess." He took her hands in his, squeezing gently.

She nodded. "I've been cranky and tired and frustrated. I have every reason, you know? Grandma's bills aren't going to pay themselves. Greg's settlement covered the first two strokes and the resulting complications and therapy, but there's nothing left, and bills keep coming in. And Cody… Ryder, I know growing up is hard, but his stutter makes it that much harder. Ms. Chavez is amazing, our new speech teacher, but it's not like his stutter is going to go away overnight. Stress can complicate it, too." She spoke quickly, her words pouring out of her. "And the job. I need this job, you know? So I assumed all of this was why I was feeling so out of sorts. But that's just not me, you know?"

He nodded.

"But there were other things…well, actually two things. I thought it was stomach flu. And then I was late. And I've never been late. Except when I found out I was expecting Cody. I wanted to pretend this wasn't happening but I'm not a coward. I had to know." Her eyes met his. "You need to know."

He couldn't breathe. He tried, but it felt like a horse had kicked him square in the chest. He knew what she was saying. Damn it.

"Ryder…" She paused. "I'm pregnant. I'm fine doing it on my own. I know now's your time to get out of Stonewall Crossing. I understand. I won't stop you. I just thought you should know—so there's some sort of plan."

"Plan?" he repeated, his mind racing. She was pregnant. He got her pregnant.

She nodded.

He stood, needing space. Her words seemed to echo in his ears. She was pregnant but didn't expect his help. That was good…wasn't it? Shit. No matter how hard he tried, he couldn't breathe. The walls were closing in, making him hot and uncomfortable. "Be right back." He hurried into the bathroom to splash some cold water on his face.

ANNABETH WATCHED HIM GO. She should have waited. She should have waited until morning, after a good night's sleep. As if she'd get any sleep.

As soon as she'd come home from work, she'd closed the bathroom door, ripped open the pregnancy test box and read the directions. Then she'd read the Spanish version of the directions, then the English version again. She'd opened the foil package holding the test and put the innocent white plastic stick on the edge of the sink. The "Results in 3 Minutes" outlined in bold was almost a threat. And three minutes later, her world changed forever.

She'd had a few hours to process it. *Superman* was a long movie. Considering what she'd told him, Ryder was handling it pretty well.

The question was simple: Would he want to be a father? But with his dream job and the promise of a new life outside Stonewall Crossing, she had her answer. And she didn't blame him—not really.

She wrinkled her nose, willing the tears back. It didn't matter. She'd been managing on her own just fine so far. She didn't, wouldn't, need him.

"I need some hot chocolate," she called out to Ryder as she headed into the kitchen. "Want some?"

He didn't answer.

She pulled the milk from her refrigerator, needing something to do while Ryder was doing whatever it was he was doing. With a few clicks, the old gas burner flamed to life. She turned it down low and poured two cups of milk into the saucepan. She opened the cabinet, moving cans and boxes until she found the hot chocolate packets.

She glanced down the hall. No Ryder. He needed time, and she'd give it to him.

The first bubbles in the milk appeared. She couldn't leave it, the milk would scorch. She stirred the milk with a wooden spoon, feeling colder with each passing second. Once the milk reached a nice rolling boil, she sprinkled in the cocoa and turned down the burner. She poured the cocoa into two mugs and carried them to the bathroom.

Ryder was bent over, his hands on his thighs. He was breathing hard, as though he'd been running for miles and couldn't catch his breath.

"Hot chocolate?" she asked, her voice sounding hollow.

He straightened, attempting his normal careless stance and cocky grin even though his skin was an alarming shade of white.

"Or something stronger?" Annabeth asked, nodding at the test on the bathroom sink. There was no mistaking the bright blue plus mark on the test window. "Definitely something stronger."

He was staring at her, his pale blue eyes so piercing it was hard not to cringe. But she didn't. She met his gaze, refusing to buckle or fall apart. The longer he stared at her, the more nervous she became. She jumped when he took the mugs from her, placing them on the bathroom counter. When he pulled her into his arms, she couldn't decide whether to brush him off or melt into him. Then he made the choice easy for her, pressing her head against his shoulder and running his fingers through her long hair.

She could hear his heart, racing like crazy, under her ear. His breath was unsteady, too. But he stood straight, holding her so close his heat warmed her. It would be easier if he didn't feel so damn good, if he didn't feel so right...

"It's late." Ryder's voice was soft, his arms slipping from her. "You... I... I should let you get some sleep."

She stepped back, grappling with his words and what they might mean. "Okay."

"Give me time...to think." He kept looking at her, his gaze wandering over her face, her stomach, before he glanced back at the test. She saw the muscle in his jaw harden, the leap of his pulse along the thick column of his tan neck. "I'll go," he added.

She stepped back, out of his way. If he wanted to leave, she wasn't going to stop him. But the look on his face, the shame and self-loathing, made her wonder if she'd ever see Ryder again.

Keep it together, Annabeth. This is best. At least she knew what to expect. The biggest surprise was how devastated she felt when he pulled the front door closed behind him, leaving her with two steaming mugs of cocoa and one bright blue pregnancy test.

RYDER SAT ON his bike, staring at the closed door of Annabeth's house.

He couldn't breathe.

He couldn't think.

A baby.

He stared up, sucking in lungfuls of bitter cold night air. A shooting star caught his eye, giving him a point of focus. He had to get his head on straight, had to think about what this...a baby...meant.

Being a parent? A father? He didn't know how to do that.

With a quick kick, his bike roared to life. He headed

straight to the gas station on the edge of town and picked up two longneck beers. After they were tucked into his saddlebag, he headed out of town.

The city had built a fence around the Stonewall Crossing cemetery after a few headstones were shot up with a pellet gun. Kids probably. His family donated the stone and wood for the decorated, and highly effective, fence that now surrounded the cemetery. It didn't stop anyone who *really* wanted in, but most kids looked for an easier target.

Ryder parked his bike, shoved the beers into the pockets of his leather jacket and jumped onto one of the four-foot-tall decorative stone posts of the fence. He gripped the top of the fence, shoved his boot into the chain link and swung himself over. The drop was a little farther than he expected, making him wince when he hit the dirt.

He paused then, his nerves unexpected.

With another deep breath, he headed across the fields. He knew where he was going, even if he hadn't been there in five years. He'd never planned on coming back. Greg sure as hell wouldn't expect him to stop by. But, damn, right now he needed his best friend.

He stood staring at the white marble headstone. He read the inscription four times before he got the nerve to step closer. *Gregory Cody Upton. Loving Husband and Father.* He'd never had a better friend—except maybe Annabeth.

Annabeth. He looked up, staring blindly at the star-laden sky.

"Hey." He cleared his throat. "Brought you something." He pulled one beer out, using his pocket knife to pop the cap off. "Figured you were going to need a drink."

He set the beer on the headstone and opened the other beer for himself, taking a healthy swig before he spoke again. He couldn't say it, not yet, so he said, "Cody's getting big. Good kid, smart as a whip. He can look at something and see the way it fits together, how it works. Bet he'll be an engineer or something. He's got Annabeth's smarts—he's gonna be a man you'd be proud of." He stooped to remove the dried leaves that piled around the base of the headstone.

When the stone was clean he sat, leaning against it as he turned his gaze back to the sky. "I need you to hear this from me." He swallowed down some beer, easing the tightening of his throat. "Annabeth—" He broke off and took another sip. "I had no right to… I… She's going to have a baby." He cleared his throat again, the press of guilt and self-loathing all but choking him. "My baby…and I'll do right by her."

He paused, closing his eyes. "You know. You know how I felt about her." He turned the bottle in his hands. "I'm not you, never will be. Cody's always gonna know who you are and what kind of man you were." He took another sip. "I'm hoping you'll be okay with them being my family now." He stared up, letting the howl of the wind fill the night.

"I'll take care of them," he promised softly. He meant it, wanted it, but had no idea where to start.

He sat there, ignoring the bitter cold, and finished his beer with his best friend.

Chapter Four

"You're sick?" Josie asked.

"Yep," Annabeth lied, pulling everything from the last kitchen cabinet. She'd been cleaning since four this morning. Her brain wouldn't turn off and she couldn't sit still. As silly as it was, she'd hoped she and Ryder would be figuring this out together. Instead, she was grappling with what to do—on her own. Her neatly color-coded poster hadn't offered much comfort this morning.

Instead of succumbing to a full-blown sob-fest, she'd busied herself. How many times had Grandma Flo told her a real lady never let her emotions run amuck? *Best use that pent-up energy to* do *something.* So all morning, she'd been *doing.* Specifically, cleaning. The tiny bathroom had been scrubbed, sterilized and organized. Her bright yellow kitchen smelled fresh, but she wouldn't be done until each and every cabinet and shelf were orderly.

"Does this have anything to do with my wayward brother-in-law's late-night visit?" Josie asked.

Annabeth dropped the can of peaches she'd been holding. "What... How..."

"Lola heard him—er, his bike."

Ryder and that damn bike. "Dammit—"

"She promised me she wouldn't tell anyone else," Josie interrupted.

"You believe her?" Annabeth knew Lola Worley far better than Josie did. While Josie was off exploring the world, Annabeth had stayed put and knew all about Lola's favorite pastime: gossip. Lola was Josie's soon-to-be step-mother, so Annabeth wasn't sure Josie could see the older woman objectively. To be fair, Lola *was* a lot less inclined to poke her nose into other peoples' business now that she had a sweetie, but...

"I do. She likes you, Annabeth. Last night's visit might be newsworthy but she'd never cause you trouble." Josie paused, then said, "I'm coming over."

"No," Annabeth pleaded. If she had a supportive shoulder to cry on, she might actually cry.

Josie argued, "It's not like you to get all hermit-like. Whatever is going on, we'll figure it out. And, if you're getting thoroughly laid, I promise not to be horrified or judgmental, okay?"

Annabeth laughed then. She couldn't help it. "Oh, Josie, I wish."

"Hmm. Okay, well, I'm coming. And I'm bringing wine." And she hung up.

"Ma?" Cody was coloring at the table. "Can I build a tree house?"

"I don't think we have a tree big enough for one, sweetie."

"'Kay," he said, the brown crayon in his hand never slowing. Tom was curled up on the table in front of Cody, his long white-tipped tail swaying back and forth with a slow, undulating rhythm.

"You want a tree house?" she asked.

"Yeah." He stopped coloring. "What about that tree?" He pointed out the small window above the kitchen sink.

"That *would* be the perfect tree for a tree house. Only problem is, it's not ours." Her gaze lingered on the empty house she'd loved since she'd come to live with Florence as a little girl. The Czinkovic house was like a dollhouse. Wraparound porches on both stories, picture windows, detailed trim-work and a massive yard with fruit and pecan trees. It was the kind of house a little girl imagined living in, with her perfect family at her side.

She glanced down at her son. All he wanted was a tree house. She wished she could give him what he wanted. After all, a tree house wasn't all that much to ask for. "If it was our house, I'd help you build one." Her gaze lingered on the house. "After we were done building your tree house, you could help me paint the big house. Maybe a dusky pink or purple—"

Cody wrinkled up his nose. "Ma! I c-can't live in a pink or p-p-purple house!"

She sat beside him, slipping an arm around him and pulling him close. "Okay, little man, what color then?"

Cody cocked his head, staring at the grand old house for a second. "Not sure," he said, dumping his box of colors onto the table. "This?" He picked up a yellow. "Your f-favor-ite."

She shrugged. "Maybe."

Cody sat it down, moving colors around until he found a pretty lilac blue. "This?"

Annabeth held it up to the window, looking at the color, then the house. "I like it, Cody. A lot."

He smiled up at her. "Is J-Josie c-coming over?"

She nodded.

"Eli, too?" he asked, smiling when Tom stirred long enough to roll onto his back.

"I don't know." Eli was Josie's stepson. He was a little older than Cody and a great kid. "How'd you like to go make cookies with Ms. Lola and Carl over at the bakery tonight?" she asked.

"Do I get to eat 'em?" he asked, grinning.

"Some of them," she relented.

"Sure." He nodded, picking up a green.

She stared at the picture her son was creating. It was a tree house, a wonderful, whimsical tree house with a ladder that wrapped around the wide trunk of the tree. "Is that an elevator?" she asked, pointing to a rope with something tied to it.

"For Tom."

She smiled, ruffling Cody's hair. She reached forward, stroking the kitten's head and ears until the purrs reverberated off the kitchen walls.

"He's h-h-happy." Cody giggled. There wasn't a sweeter sound in her world.

"What's not to be happy about? He's got you and me, kiddo. He's one lucky kitten."

Tom mewed faintly, making them both smile.

"Think that means he agrees?" she asked Cody.

"Yep." Cody nodded.

She pressed a kiss to his head, breathing in his sweet scent, his soft hair tickling her nose. Cody was her boy, the reason she worked so hard each and every day. He was thoughtful and considerate, funny and kind. She was proud of him.

"Here." Cody handed her a green crayon and pointed at the base of the tree. "Some grass?"

She started to color, a companionable silence filling the small kitchen. She loved these quiet times, just the two of them. Tom mewed, making her smile. *Fine, three of us…* But starting over again terrified her.

Cody was made from solid love. When she'd found out she was expecting Cody, she'd thought Greg would be there to help out. Greg had been so excited about a baby, even more so when he found out they were having a son. There'd been the promise of a family, happy and whole.

Cody's smile was Greg's. So were the kinks in his little toes. She couldn't help but think of Greg each and every time she saw Cody barefoot. It used to tear her up inside, but now it made her smile. Greg was a good man, a good husband. Even though he never met his son, Annabeth knew he'd left the best parts of himself here in Cody.

This baby… Ryder's baby. She drew in a deep breath. Poor little thing was made in a truck, clumsy and hurried and, honestly, a mistake. It wasn't the beginning she would have imagined for her child, if she'd imagined having another child—which she hadn't.

She'd had a hard time imagining sex, let alone the possible consequences. Greg was the only man she'd slept with. So sex, without Greg, was a foreign concept. It hadn't always been perfect, but they'd had the time to learn each other's bodies, to give each other real pleasure. The exact opposite of what happened with Ryder. They'd had no time, no experience and no hesitation. And yet somehow it had been one of the most intense experiences of her life.

"Nice," Cody said, smiling up at her. "You can make some f-flowers if you want."

She should be enjoying time with Cody, not thinking about her love life. Or, more accurately, her lack of a love life. This baby was coming. There was no way to make this okay, but there had to be a way to make it less of a mess than it was.

There was a knock on the door. "Hello?" Josie called out.

"Come in," Annabeth answered.

Eli, Josie and Hunter all spilled into her small kitchen. Seeing Hunter, the eldest Boone sibling, made her think about Ryder and the mess she was in.

"Hey." Annabeth stood, tugging her giant sweatshirt past her hips. She hadn't bothered to put herself together today. Now she was acutely aware of her oversize sweats and sloppy ponytail. Not that she had time to worry about it too much. Hunter had the boys bundled up and out the door, "to a livestock auction for some man time," before she'd said more than a dozen words. It was only when she and Josie were left alone in the kitchen that she noticed the way Josie was looking at her.

"What?" Annabeth asked.

"What's up?" Josie asked, opening the cabinets and taking in the morning cleaning spree.

"Nothing—"

"Don't tell me nothing." Josie smiled at her. "I know about the job. And I know Flo's hospital bills still exist. And I know Cody's getting grief at school, but this is something else."

Annabeth started packing up Cody's crayons. "Why does there have to be something else?"

"Because Annabeth Upton gets dressed every day. She puts on her makeup, does her hair and believes you fake it 'til you make it. Your mantra is 'make lemonade out of the lemons life gives you' so…yes, there has to be something else." Josie put her hands on her hips. "Don't get me wrong, I think you're crazy for always being so together, but this—" she pointed at Annabeth "—isn't you."

Annabeth slid into the kitchen chair, watching Tom bat one of the crayons across the table and onto the floor.

"*Is* it Ryder?" Josie rifled through the cabinets until she found two empty glass Mason jars. "You're one of the only people he talks to, you know that? When he comes out to the ranch, he's still so distant."

"He still blames himself," Annabeth spoke softly.

"For?"

"His mother's death." She'd never forget how devastated he was.

Sophomore year Ryder was already a hell-raiser. His

mom had gone to pick him up after he'd snuck out and drunk too much to drive home. She'd swerved to avoid a deer and the car had landed upside down in a ditch. Ryder had cut through her seat belt to get her out, but he couldn't resuscitate her. His father shut down for almost a year, leaving Hunter to pick up the pieces. Ryder took the blame—and more risks than ever. Starting fights, run-ins with the law—and nothing she or Greg said had helped. But whether it was the guilt and anger eating him or the need for his father's attention that drove him to such measures, Annabeth wasn't sure.

"It wasn't his fault." Josie frowned.

"I think everyone knows that except Ryder. And, maybe, his father."

Josie's frown grew. "Teddy blames him?"

She shrugged. "Ryder thinks he does. And Ryder does. And that's all that matters."

"That's what I'm talking about. You're the only one that knows that." Josie shook her head. "That thing—that connection—you two have."

"What?" Annabeth looked up. "What thing?"

"Oh, please." Josie opened the bottle of wine she'd carried in and filled both glasses halfway.

"Seriously," Annabeth pushed. "What thing?"

Josie sat across from her, a confused look on her face. "I always got the impression you two were hot for each other. Even in high school, there was that—zing." She paused. "Not that either of you acted on it. Greg was there."

Annabeth stared at the wine in the Mason jar, wishing she could drink it but knowing she wouldn't. "Well, we did."

Josie almost snorted her wine.

"And I'm pregnant."

Josie started coughing.

"And I don't think he's interested in being a father." Annabeth stood, getting a glass of water for Josie.

Josie took a long sip, stared at Annabeth then took a long sip of her wine.

"Exactly." Annabeth nodded.

Josie sat her glass down, collecting her thoughts. "What's the plan?" Josie finally asked.

She thought of the poster in her room. "I'm not sure," she admitted. "I have… I have a chart—" She broke off.

Josie took Annabeth's hands in hers. "Oh, sweetie, we'll figure it out."

Annabeth nodded, refusing to give in and cry.

"FLO SAID TO tell you she's in a meeting," the nurse said, a tolerant smile on her face. "I'm sure she'll be done soon. She likes to exert a little power now and then."

Ryder nodded, tucking the box of chocolates under his arm. "Who doesn't? I'll let her finish up." He winked at the pretty nurse, watching her flush in response. Yesterday, he'd have asked for her number. But yesterday was another life. Now, this life, was all about being responsible. He was going to do what he should do—for Annabeth, Cody and his baby. The first step was getting permission from Annabeth's family—Flo.

"You can send him in, Nancy," Flo called loudly from her room.

Ryder touched the rim of his hat at Nancy and entered the bedroom where Florence Chenault lived. Every inch of wall space was dotted with newspaper clippings, drawings and framed photos. A tall wooden dresser filled one corner of the room, standing out amongst the other institutional-grade furniture. The single bed was covered in quilts and a chenille sweater. Flo sat in her wheelchair, wearing a green velvet robe and her hair in a fancy updo.

"You're a fine sight," Ryder said, offering her the box of chocolates.

Flo grinned. "And you, Ryder Boone, are a scamp."

"Guilty." He hugged her, dropping a kiss on her cheek.

She opened the box of chocolates and offered it to him. "Go on."

"I got it for you," he argued.

"Uh-huh." She placed the box in her lap, popping a candy into her mouth before adding, "And when a scamp shows up with gifts, it means he's after something."

"Known a lot of scamps?"

She smiled sweetly. "I have, young man, I have indeed. Your father was one of them." She patted the corner of her bed. "You sit a spell and tell me what you're after."

Ryder sat, placing his hat on the bed beside him. "Annabeth—"

"It's about time," Flo cut in, her eyes fixed on his face. "You going to make an honest woman out of her?"

Ryder swallowed. "If she'll have me."

She nodded. "Open that top drawer." She pointed at the dresser in the corner. "In the little blue box in the back corner. Careful, it's breakable."

Ryder did as he was told, lifting the blue porcelain box and carrying it to Flo.

"Open it." Flo waved her hand at him. "My hands get so shaky sometimes."

Ryder's hands weren't all that steady either, but he opened the box.

"Those belonged to Annabeth's parents," Flo said.

Ryder stared at the three rings inside. One was a bridal set, slim and delicate, with a large round diamond. The other was a wide gold band, the word *Forever* etched on the inside of both bands.

"Hannah wanted Annabeth to have these, but Greg

didn't want 'em. You don't have to use them, either." Flo paused. "Seems like maybe they'd bring you two luck, since Michael and Hannah loved each other so." She pointed to the rings. "Not that you two are going to need any luck, Ryder. You two are the only ones that don't see how you fit together."

"You think so?" He wanted to believe her.

She nodded, reaching forward to pat his hand. "She loves you, Ryder Boone. Whether that silly, stubborn girl sees it or not."

"She is stubborn." That much he agreed on.

"A real man never speaks ill of his woman, remember that." Flo frowned. "You better treat her right, you hear me? If you don't, I will come back from the grave and drive you crazy with haunting."

"Does this mean I have your blessing?" he asked.

"I'm a mite disappointed you've waited so long, I'll be honest." She sat back in her chair, narrowing her eyes a bit. "First, you tell me why you want to marry my girl, why you deserve her, and we'll see."

He swallowed, knowing the truth wasn't the right way to go. "She's Annabeth, Flo. Guess I've come to realize what a...an amazing woman she is."

"Mmm-hmm." Flo's eyebrows went up.

"If you're looking for poems and pretty words, I'm going to disappoint you." He chuckled. "I might be good at charming the pants off a woman, but courting's another thing."

Flo popped another chocolate into her mouth. "Try."

He shook his head, staring out the window. He knew Flo wasn't trying to irritate him. She had every right to make sure he was worthy of Annabeth. Problem was, he knew he wasn't. His words were rushed. "You want me to tell you she's smart and sassy? That she's so damn pretty sometimes it hurts to look at her? Or making her smile makes a shi— A bad day good?" His throat felt tight, his palms sweaty… "I don't deserve her. But I'll try to. Every damn day." Tripping over his words was nothing new. He could only hope he'd manage the right ones when he was on his knee in front of Annabeth. He looked at Flo, staring at the box of chocolates in her lap. "Flo?"

"You'll do just fine." Her smile wavered, her gaze wandering out the large window in her room. "But marry my girl soon. Hannah wouldn't be much good without you, Michael."

Ryder nodded, sad that Flo was gone.

"Now that you have a baby on the way, you need to be more careful," Flo added. This was news to Ryder. Had Annabeth's parents been in the same position he and Annabeth were in? Flo continued, "You drive too fast. Man wasn't meant to zoom around going eighty miles an hour in big metal cans. Slow down, son, take time to stop and smell the roses. Make some memories to treasure. Life goes by too quick, I promise you. It's your memories that will keep you company long after everyone else is gone."

Ryder nodded again, wondering if Flo had said as much to Michael. Annabeth's parents died in a car crash. "I promise." And he meant it. She might be talking to Michael, but he'd take her advice to heart. "I'll take good care of her."

Flo nodded. "She's my only baby, my joy. See that you do."

He didn't know the little person growing inside of Annabeth, but he knew the baby was his. And, in the past twelve hours, he'd come to terms with that. It twisted his heart to think of the loss Flo had lived through. Hannah had been her only child, Annabeth her only grandchild.

"Mrs. Chenault?" Nancy came in, small white cup in hand. "We have your vitamins."

"Oh, goodie." Flo's voice dripped with sarcasm. "They keep telling me these are vitamins, like I don't know better?" She rolled her eyes—just like Annabeth.

Ryder smiled.

"Then we have our backgammon tournament," Nancy continued.

"Is that today?" Flo perked up. "We'll have to wrap this up, Michael."

"Yes, ma'am." He stood, tucking the rings into his jeans pocket and putting on his hat. "I'll go take care of my business, you go kick some backgammon butt."

"Oh, I will." She giggled, waving a quick goodbye before Nancy wheeled her in the direction of the activity center.

He couldn't go to Annabeth's house, not yet. His talk with Flo had put things in perspective. He couldn't just drop by and ask her, straight out. If he was going to do it right, he needed to go home, clean up and think about what he was going to say. There was no doubt some arguing and rationalizing would be involved—Annabeth was good at that. So he had to be ready for whatever roadblock she might throw up and somehow manage to make it special.

But he didn't stop at his small apartment over Hardy's Garage. He kept driving, past the garage, past the school and Annabeth's street, down Main Street. It was only as he turned his truck under the stone-and-wrought-iron entrance that he realized he was heading home to Boone Ranch.

He parked his truck in front of the Lodge, the bed-and-breakfast his father had operated and lived in for the past few years. Why he'd ended up here was a mystery. The last thing he wanted was one of his father's disappointed looks or loaded silences. His father spoke volumes with a simple shake of his head. So why had he come here? He could go. No one knew he was here. But he knew.

He opened the truck door and climbed the steps, nodding at the group of visitors assembling for the night's stargazing tour. It was one of the diversions his father had dreamed up for his guests. Bird-watching, nature photography and trail riding were others. Between Hunter's efforts to work with the state on white-tailed and exotic deer population studies and Archer's neighboring animal refuge, guests were treated to an almost safari-like experience. And people loved it, flocking from all over the country to visit Texas and stay on a working ranch. A ranch with every amenity and world-class cooking.

He stepped inside, dodging his nephew, Eli, as he ran by. Cody followed, laughing. The tantalizing scent of freshly baked cookies reached him.

"Eight, nine, ten," his sister Renata's voice echoed. "Ten more, boys."

He checked his boots for mud, rested his hat on the hat tree and his coat on the peg beneath before heading into the great room. His father sat before the fire, his reading glasses perched on the end of his nose as he read over some ranching magazine. Seeing his father never failed to stir up years of self-doubt best left ignored. Or to remind him of his part in his mother's death. He swallowed, speaking gruffly. "Dad."

His father's brows dipped as he set aside his magazine. "Ryder." He stood, tucking his glasses into his pocket. "Good to see you, son."

Ryder nodded.

Renata ran into the great room. "Ready or not, here I come... Hey, baby brother." She hugged him, pressing a kiss to his cheek. "Off to find some rug rats."

"Have fun." He smiled.

"Don't eat all the cookies," she chastised before heading out.

"I'll try," he answered, aware his father was watching him. His unannounced arrival was suspect. He didn't *drop by*. Hell, he had no idea *why* he was here. But he was.

"Hunter here?" Ryder asked.

"Looking for him?" his father countered.

"Not really, why?"

His father shook his head, waving him into the kitchen. "Lola and Carl dropped the boys off earlier, after feeding 'em a bag of sugar each from the looks of it. But there might be some cookies left over in here, if you want."

Ryder nodded, following his father into the kitchen. Hunter was washing dishes, a towel thrown over his shoulder.

"She found 'em yet?" Hunter asked.

"No, but I found something," his father said.

Hunter turned, smiling. "Hey."

"Look how domestic you are," Ryder teased. "And it's only been, what, two months?"

Hunter shook his head. "Jealous?"

Ryder arched an eyebrow at his brother and stuffed a cookie into his mouth.

"How's John? Anything new at the garage?" Hunter asked.

Ryder shrugged. "Been pretty steady since the storm. Mostly weatherizing though."

"Nothing to sink your chops into?" His father smiled.

Ryder shrugged.

"Heard you were on the circuit for a bit, how you took a nasty spill. Glad to see you're no worse for wear." His father had always hated Ryder's rodeoing. Teddy Boone believed in hard work, responsibility and family. Sometimes Ryder wondered, if he hadn't torn their family apart, would he see respect in his father's eyes instead of wariness and disappointment? He'd never know.

He watched his father move around the kitchen, spry and agile. "Ride times good?" His father offered him a large glass of milk.

Ryder nodded.

"How'd you do?" Hunter asked.

Ryder shrugged.

Hunter laughed, shaking his head.

A squeal from the other room made all three of them jump.

"Found you, Eli!" Renata laughed. "You can come out, Cody. Eli's it."

A small stampede of footsteps announced their return.

"Hey, R-Ryder." Cody smiled. "Good?" he asked as Ryder shoved another cookie in his mouth.

"Snickerdoodles are his favorite." Renata nudged him in the side.

"Mine, too," Cody said, grinning.

"Smart kid." Ryder winked at him.

Cody's ear-to-ear smile looked so much like Greg's it took his breath away. There were days he missed Greg, his no-nonsense take on life, and their easy camaraderie. It was bittersweet, to see his best friend so clearly in this little boy. A little boy who'd never know his father. The little boy who, if he could convince Annabeth they could make it work, would be his stepson. Cody would be a great big brother to the baby...a son he'd be proud of. He ruffled the boy's hair, resisting the sudden urge to hug him. "Having a good time?" he asked.

Cody nodded.

"Annabeth was under the weather, so Josie went over to

cheer her up," Hunter offered. "We figured Cody'd have more fun here."

Ryder frowned. Annabeth wasn't feeling well? He should know this, should be taking care of her. "She okay?" he asked before he could stop himself. He didn't miss the slight narrowing of Hunter's eyes.

Cody shrugged. "She said she was tired."

"You ready to hide?" Eli asked Cody.

"Last time," Hunter said, though his attention never wandered from Ryder. "We'll take Cody on home and pick up Jo before it gets too late."

Renata and Cody ran off while Eli started counting in the great room.

Hunter cast a quick glance at their father before adding, "You ready to tell us why you're here?"

Ryder cocked an eyebrow. "Why does there have to be a reason?"

"You gonna stop using questions as your answers?" his father interjected.

Ryder and Hunter laughed then. Ever since Ryder was a boy, he'd answer questions with questions to muddy the waters—hoping to avoid trouble or consequences. It had irritated their father to no end.

"You in trouble?" his father asked.

Ryder opened his mouth, ready to answer with some smart-ass comeback. Assuming Ryder was in trouble would be the first conclusion his father would jump to. And, even though his father was right, he couldn't dismiss the anger his father's question stirred up.

"Ryder?" his father repeated.

"No, sir," he answered. "On my way to Fisher's for my steel-toe boots," he lied.

His father frowned while Hunter crossed his arms over his chest, waiting.

"I can't just stop by?" Ryder felt his cheeks burn, the words damn near choking him.

His father stared at him, long and hard. "'Course you can, Ryder. This is your home."

"Might stop by more often for these," he murmured, holding up a snickerdoodle cookie.

There was a loud thump, sending their father out of the kitchen with a smile, and leaving Ryder alone with his big brother.

"'Fess up." Hunter's voice was low, neutral.

Ryder placed his half-eaten cookie back on the plate.

"I'm thinking it's the same girl that's had you wrapped around her pinkie since grade school."

Ryder couldn't help grinning.

Hunter sighed. "Jo thinks something's going on between you and Annabeth."

Ryder met his brother's stare.

"Then you're one lucky son of a bitch." Hunter stared at him, long and hard. "But she and Cody have been through a lot. She comes with a kid, a big job, her grandmother… Makes things harder, when so many people are involved, if things don't work out. A lot of people can get hurt. Like me and Amy—a lot of hurt there." Hunter shook his head. "I was damn lucky to get a second chance with Jo."

"Guess I was hoping not to talk about the end of something that hasn't started yet." Ryder felt his temper rising. His brother's mess of a first marriage and nasty divorce was nothing like what he and Annabeth were facing. Yes, he'd messed up more times than not, but—just once—it'd be nice not to get a lecture from his family.

Hunter nodded. "Just don't screw things up."

"I don't plan on it." Ryder sighed, his chest heavy. "But it'd be a hell of a lot easier if I knew what to do next."

"Start with telling her how you feel. Then show her

what she means to you." Hunter grinned. "Then do it again, every day."

Hearing his brother say it out loud made it sound easy. He suspected it wasn't, but at least now he had a place to start. It was something he'd make damn sure he stayed on top of. Ryder picked up the cookie and popped it into his mouth.

Chapter Five

Annabeth parked her car and rested her head on the steering wheel. This had been one of her all-time longest days—wrapping up one of the longest weeks of her life. She'd been so busy she'd lost track of time. Once Greg's parents had picked up Cody from school, she'd had team meetings, campus improvement council and a mountain of certificates to review and sign before the academic awards ceremony next week.

This weekend she planned on sleeping, if she wasn't too nauseous. She'd never once thrown up when she was expecting Cody, but she'd been fighting to keep every bite down for the past few days. She'd gone through an entire box of crackers and a few bottles of ginger ale, but neither had done much good.

She turned off Lady Blue and climbed out of the car, tugging her briefcase and laptop bag out with her. It was only as she opened the door that she realized the front porch light was on. And the kitchen light was on. And music was playing.

"Hello?" she called out, too exhausted to be scared. It was Stonewall Crossing, after all—folks looked out for each other. If she had something to worry about, one of her neighbors would have let her know.

Ryder walked out of the kitchen, all smiles. Her lime-green-and-lemon-yellow-pattern apron looked downright sexy over his skintight black T-shirt and jeans. "You work long hours, Princess."

She stood frozen, surprised, as he took her bags and helped her out of her coat. His thumb brushed the base of her neck, sending a shiver down her spine and jolting her into action. "Cody's spending the weekend with Greg's folks, so I wanted to wrap up all the loose ends before I left." She followed him, unable to resist the view of his perfect butt encased in snug, work-worn jeans. "A little surprised to see you here—" Her stomach roiled as the mingling scents of garlic, rosemary, and…freesia filled her nostrils. She pressed her hand over her mouth and swallowed.

"You okay?" His smile dimmed as he looked at her. "You look a little green."

She shook her head, swallowing repeatedly, as she stared around the kitchen. The small table was covered in her best tablecloth and set with her mother's china. Candles flickered invitingly beside a massive bouquet of flowers. And a bottle of sparkling grape juice sat beside two wineglasses on the counter. "What's this?" she murmured.

"Dinner." He pulled a chair back for her.

She cocked an eyebrow at him, too bewildered—and tired—to argue. She sat, her mind racing. She should be mad at him. She should be yelling at him for running for the hills. She should kick him out and crawl into bed. But she was too tired. All she managed was "Why are you cooking me dinner?"

"To apologize." The uncertainty in his voice drew her full attention. She'd never seen him look so…nervous. Her stomach tightened, apprehension filling her.

"For?" She forced the words out.

"Acting like a dick." He knelt in front of her, taking both her hands in his. "You deserve better, we both know that."

She was speechless.

"It's not like we're strangers."

She opened her mouth, but nothing came out.

"You and Cody are important to me. You always have been." He cleared his throat. "Let me take care of you?"

Important to him. She knew that. She knew he would be there if she needed him. "Ryder..." Her voice was husky. She pulled one of her hands from his to take a sip of water. "What are you saying?" Her head was spinning. "Exactly?"

"Marry me." His gaze traveled over her face. "Will you marry me?"

Marry him? "What?" she croaked. Emotion and nausea had her stomach churning.

He smiled. "You heard me."

"I did, but..." She shook her head, then nodded. "Why? You don't want this—"

"I might have not have known it a week ago, but yeah, I do want this." His hand cupped her cheek, his voice warm and sincere. "We'll be good together, Princess. You might have to—" The stove timer beeped and Ryder jumped up, opening the oven to pull out whatever was cooking. The scent of garlic quadrupled, and her stomach clenched violently as Ryder placed a pan of lasagna on the plate trivet in front of her.

"Oh, God." She covered her mouth. She was not going to toss her cookies in the middle of Ryder's proposal. She stood, ready to run for the bathroom.

"Annabeth..." The anguish in his voice made her pause.

Here was this gorgeous man, wearing her apron and mismatched oven mitts, cooking a romantic dinner for them…asking her to marry him. And her stomach was going to rebel any second.

"I need a minute." She held up a finger.

"I know I ran out on you, but I won't ever do it again." He threw the oven mitts over his shoulders, crossed the room in two big steps and gripped her shoulders. "I don't mind spending all night convincing you how right we are," he murmured, drawing her close as he bent his head.

Oh no. "Ryder, stop!" She pushed against his wall of a chest right before she threw up all over the kitchen floor.

RYDER KNEW NOW was not the time to laugh. But, damn, it took everything he had not to. One look at her horrified expression and he couldn't resist a slight chuckle. "Is it me?" he teased.

She scowled at him. "You could say that." She pointed to her stomach.

For some reason, that made him laugh. "Already causing trouble."

She sighed, stepping away from the mess on the floor. "I'll get the mop."

"You lie down. I'll clean this up."

She stared at him, so tired and frail looking his heart hurt. "I can do it, Ryder."

"You can." He sighed, stepping over the mess. "But you don't have to. I've got this."

She frowned at him but didn't fight as he led her to her bedroom. She sat on the edge of the bed, too pale for his liking. He knelt to remove her boots. His fingers stroked along her calf before pulling her foot free. He smiled as she stretched and wiggled her toes. It was impossible not to stroke the arch of her left foot, to resist touching her. He looked up, swallowing at the sight that greeted him.

Annabeth's eyes were closed, her toes arching as he

massaged her foot. She looked sexy as hell, her fingers gripping the quilt, the slight part of her lips, and hiss of her breathing. He could imagine laying her back on the big, empty bed and worshipping every inch of her. He drew in a deep breath. Now wasn't the time. Instead, he pulled off her other boot and kneaded her foot until she groaned.

"I'm not tired," she murmured.

He released her foot and stood, freeing her golden hair from its long braid. She could barely keep her eyes open. "Sure you're not."

Her hazel eyes met his. "I need to take a shower first."

He forced himself to walk the few steps from her small bedroom to the tiny bathroom. After he'd cleared an army of bath toys from the tub, he filled it with warm water and lemon-scented bubbles. Annabeth-scented bubbles.

He poked his head into her bedroom to find her sitting in exactly the same place. She was staring at the floor, looking deflated. "Bubble bath's ready."

Her surprise was evident, but her delighted smile was huge. "Thank you."

He winked at her, wishing there was more he could do. How was he going to convince her he'd take some of the weight off her shoulders? He had no idea.

Once she'd closed the bathroom door behind her, he cleaned up the kitchen floor and sealed the lasagna and garlic bread in a Tupperware container. When that was done, he paced the length of the house. This wasn't exactly the way he'd pictured tonight. But she hadn't turned him down, not yet.

"You're going to wear a hole through the wood floor," Annabeth called from the bathroom.

"I can fix that," he called back.

Her laugh made him smile.

A few minutes later, he heard the whirring of an electric

toothbrush, then the bathroom door opened. She stood, hair twisted up in a towel on her head, in her rainbow pajamas.

"I'm thinking you're not hungry?" he asked.

She shook her head.

He took her hand and led her to her room. When she was sitting on the edge of her bed, he started drying her hair with the towel. "Brush?" he asked.

She rolled her eyes but pointed at the dresser.

He grabbed her brush, gently working any snarls or tangles from her long hair. "Feeling better?"

"Ugh."

He grinned, setting the brush aside. "Need anything?"

"Sleep," she said, breaking into a yawn.

He wasn't about to let her go to sleep just yet. His plans of seduction might be out the window, but he'd convinced the justice of the peace to marry them tomorrow morning. Now all he had to do was convince the bride.

He knelt in front of Annabeth, pulling the rings from his pocket.

Her eyes went round. "Where did you get these?"

"Flo." He smiled. "Wouldn't be right without her blessing."

She shook her head, the unmistakable sheen of tears in her eyes.

"Don't you cry on me, Princess." He took her left hand and slid the engagement ring on. "Just say you'll marry me. And then I'll let you get some sleep."

She stared at the ring, blinking furiously. When she looked at him, he wasn't prepared for the raw emotion lining her face. He didn't like seeing her vulnerable or afraid. He didn't like her fragile. She was the strongest person he knew.

"And if I say no?" It was a whisper.

"You can't." He hadn't expected the sharp stab of pain.

"How hard have you fought for this job? You deserve to keep it. Marrying me makes this baby a good thing instead of a liability."

He saw her bite her lip before she asked, "So you're doing this for me?"

"I'm doing this for us." He sighed. "Marry me. Tomorrow."

"Tomorrow?" Her eyes went round.

"I figured the sooner, the better. Unless you want a big wedding?"

She shook her head. "God no, but we can't do this willy-nilly—"

"Did you just say 'willy-nilly'?" He laughed.

"We need a plan, Ryder," she continued.

"Fine. *After* the ceremony. The JP owes me a favor." He waited, watching the shift of emotions on her face. "No fuss, no stress, just you and me."

Her eyes locked with his as a long stretch of silence filled the room. He wanted to pull her into his arms, to reassure her that everything was going to be okay. He wanted to kiss her. Damn, he wanted her. But more than anything, he wanted to hear her say yes.

She nodded.

"Yes?" He hadn't realized he'd been holding his breath.

"Yes." She stared down at their joined hands. "I... I know you're making sure there's no *scandal* for me and Cody and the...baby to deal with. I won't ask you to give up your life because we...were careless." She pulled her hand from his and scooted back on her bed to lie down. She didn't look at him, even though he was staring at her. Anxiety coiled in his stomach as she continued, "Before things get too complicated, we'll come up with a solid plan—so things go smoothly until we... Until it's time to divorce."

"Annabeth," he murmured, lying down on his side to

face her. His chest hurt, a pain he'd never felt before. "I'm not asking for anything half-assed." And he sure as hell didn't like how willing she was to let go of what he was offering.

She smoothed the hair from his forehead, a slight smile on her lips. Her touch left him breathless. "How many times have you said it, Ryder Boone? You're not the forever type." Her voice trailed off and her eyes closed. "But you are a good man. And a real friend."

He was an idiot. Hearing his careless words from her lips only confirmed that. Amazing how much a week could change a man's perspective on life. Forever had never included Annabeth before. He wanted Annabeth to rely on him, to count on him. He wanted to be there for her, Cody and their baby. It would take time to convince her he was in this for the long haul, but he had time. Sure, this might put his plans with JJ on hold, but his child came first.

One look at her told him how exhausted she was. She'd said yes—it was a start. She had every right to doubt him. Actions spoke louder than words. Hunter's words replayed through his head. He'd find a way to show Annabeth he was serious about this.

She sighed, her hand falling to rest on her stomach as she rolled onto her back. He stared at her hand, then covered it with his own. A baby. His baby. He had all the motivation he needed right here. The baby. Cody. Annabeth... A family. His family. Was he scared? Hell, yes. For the first time in his life, he had something to lose. He'd let her make her plan, but his wasn't going to change. He was in this, for real, for life.

Chapter Six

"Congratulations, Mr. and Mrs. Boone." Mack McCoy smiled at her.

Annabeth Boone. She was Annabeth Boone.

"You're a lucky man, Ryder." Mack shook his hand.

Right now, that's exactly how she was feeling. *She* was lucky. If Ryder hadn't proposed, what would she have done? Would she have asked for his help, like Josie suggested? Or would she have tucked tail and run to her in-laws' place? Would they take her in? It's not like this baby had anything to do with them. But, thanks to Ryder, nothing had to change…for now.

"I am." Ryder pulled her close, planting a soft kiss on her mouth before she could respond. Her body, on the other hand, was definitely reacting to his touch. Being close to him seemed to light an instant fire inside her. Waking up next to him, wrapped in his scent and warmth and arms, felt too good. So good, she'd lain there until he'd woken up. Even then, she'd have happily stayed cocooned against him. But he'd hustled her from the bed and to the justice of the peace.

Now she stood, wearing a cream sweater and jeans, married to the *rebel* Boone.

Mr. McCoy laughed, handing her the wedding certificate in its faux-leather holder. "Not to rush you two, but the missus has a honey-do list a mile long waiting for me at home." He winked. "I imagine the two of you have your own plans for the day."

She focused on the certificate she held, not the mix of emotions Mack McCoy's teasing caused. Ryder had made it clear he wasn't attracted to her from the beginning. If it hadn't been for Mr. Ego at the bar, he wouldn't have pretended he was, and she wouldn't have jumped him... For all she knew, their time together hadn't been anything special for him. Considering he'd all but bolted out of the bed when he woke up this morning, she didn't think his interest level had changed.

The smart thing to do, the thing she was best at, was focusing on the positive. And, right now, she had a lot to be positive about.

"Appreciate you coming in on your day off." Ryder nodded.

"Yes, thank you," she agreed.

"You can name one of your kids after me and we'll call it even." Mack McCoy smiled. "Middle name is Joshua, just in case you don't like Mack."

She smiled, trying to find something to say. She'd been a little tongue-tied all morning, ever since she'd woken up with her cheek on Ryder's bare chest, wrapped in his rock-hard arms.

"Morning, Mack." Renata Boone's singsong voice startled them all. "Saw your truck was out front so I thought I'd drop off those new tourism department brochures."

They hadn't really talked about how they were sharing their news with everyone. They hadn't really talked about a *lot* of things. And now Ryder's sister was here, staring at them in total confusion. "What's happening?" Renata asked.

"Give your brother a hug, Renata. It's not every day a man gets hitched." Mack clapped Ryder on the shoulder.

"What?" Renata's blue eyes went round. "Married?"

Annabeth waited, smiling what she hoped was a suitably excited smile.

Renata squealed, tossed the fliers she was holding onto the entry desk and hugged her brother. "It's about time. I thought you'd never get the nerve up to ask her."

Annabeth shot Ryder a look. He shrugged, hugging his sister. "You can't rush these things."

"Then why are you marrying her at the justice of the peace?" Renata let go of her brother and pulled Annabeth into a strong hug. "I'll have to apologize for my brother, Annabeth. He's not exactly a pro when it comes to romance."

"No." Annabeth smiled. "I liked the idea. Getting married here."

"You did?" Renata asked.

"I've done the whole wedding thing," Annabeth answered honestly. Even without the rush to the altar, she wouldn't have wanted another big wedding. "I'm more interested in being married." Married, to a partner, a friend, someone to rely on. She looked at Ryder, unnerved by the intensity in his pale blue eyes.

"When you put it that way, it makes perfect sense." Renata smiled.

Annabeth didn't resist leaning into Ryder when he slipped his arm around her waist. If anything, she wanted his support.

"You tell Dad?" Renata asked.

Ryder laughed. "It just happened."

"Normally the family knows before it *happens*," Renata argued. "You two might be fine without all the ceremony, but this town isn't going to let that happen."

Ryder shook his head. "Renata."

"Come on, Ryder." Renata frowned. "Annabeth's the principal of the elementary school. You're a Boone, your family built this town. There has to be a celebration. People will think it's weird if we don't."

She has a point. "I don't see the harm in a little get-together," Annabeth agreed, shooting for enthusiasm. "Then we can tell everyone at once." She smiled up at Ryder.

Ryder wasn't sold on the idea. "You sure?" he asked.

She nodded.

"Nothing too big, I promise," Renata went on. "I'll take care of everything, don't you worry. We'll just open up the Lodge, invite...everyone."

"Everyone?" Ryder asked.

Annabeth's stomach rumbled, sudden nausea rising up.

"Didn't you feed her before you came?" Renata asked. "Ryder Boone, you've spent too many years being doe-eyed over Annabeth. Now that you've got her, you better take care of her. You two go on and I'll call you later, once everything's set." She paused, winking. "Maybe I'll wait and call you tomorrow."

Ryder Boone had *never* been doe-eyed, ever. But Annabeth was surprised by the pleasure Renata's words gave her. She only had a few seconds to glance at Ryder—before being engulfed in another of Renata's hugs—but there was no missing the color on his cheeks. Or the tightness in his jaw. Either he was irritated by his sister's teasing or... No, he had not and would never be sweet on her. They were—and always had been—just friends. She thanked Mack McCoy and let Ryder lead her out of the small building.

"I can tell Renata to cancel the party, if you want?" Ryder offered.

Annabeth glanced at him. "If you don't want to—"

"Didn't mean that." He smiled. "I can see that brain of yours working. Guess there's a lot we need to talk about, huh?"

"The list keeps getting longer," she agreed.

"Think you can stomach some pancakes or something first?"

Pancakes sounded good. "I'll try."

He took her hand in his and led her down the brick sidewalk toward Pop's Bakery. "Might as well let Lola and Carl know, too. Between them and my sister, Stonewall Crossing will know you're my wife before we're done eating."

Wife. "Ryder," she murmured, pulling against him.

"What's wrong, Princess?" His pale blue eyes bore into hers.

"It's a lot," she murmured, trying not to get distracted by the heat in his gaze...or the memory of the way he looked tousled and shirtless in her bed. "All of it."

"I know." His attention lingered on the ring on his left hand. "Let's eat and go home."

They hadn't discussed that, either. "Home as in my place? Or home as in your apartment? Or, are you... If you don't want..." She cleared her throat. "You don't have to stay with me—"

He frowned. "The apartment won't hold you, Cody and the baby."

She looked around them, panicked that someone might hear him.

"Seems pretty pointless to get hitched if we're not sleeping under the same roof."

He shoved his hands in his pockets and stared down the street. "So I'll be staying with you. Even if you'd rather I slept on the couch."

He was right. In a town the size of Stonewall Crossing, there was no such thing as privacy or personal business. If their lightning-fast wedding didn't cause a wave a gossip, the two of them living apart immediately after the wedding surely would.

"You're right," she murmured, confused and anxious.

Ryder's pale blue eyes swept over her, the muscle in his jaw clenching briefly. "Still hungry?" His gaze was intense, further rattling her.

The knots in her stomach tightened. The last thing she meant to do was make him angry. But she'd gotten good at being on her own. Relying on him meant opening herself up, being vulnerable. She tried to explain. "Like I said, it's a lot. I've been on my own for almost six years now—"

"You're not alone anymore, got it?" he argued, his gaze falling to the sidewalk at their feet.

Maybe not right now. She wasn't the only one whose world had been turned upside down overnight. He'd done everything he could to help, and she was holding him at arm's length. "Got it." He was frustrated and angry—and he looked adorable. There was no way she could stop the smile from spreading across her face. "I'm sorry." She stepped forward, forcing him to look at her.

His gaze met hers as he let out a deep breath. The corner of his baby blues crinkled as he smiled. He shook his head at her, tugged her coat closed, and took her hand in his.

"You're kinda cute when you're angry, Ryder Boone," she admitted.

He looked at her, one eyebrow cocked. "Hell, I'm cute all the time, Princess."

She laughed, letting him lead her down Main Street to Pop's Bakery.

RYDER'S PHONE WAS ringing before they reached the bakery. It was Hunter. And Hunter was the only one he didn't want to talk to right now. He loved his big brother, but he'd be less likely to get all warm and fuzzy over his unexpected marriage than his sister.

"Need to get that?" Annabeth asked.

He shook his head. "Nope." He silenced his phone and tucked it into his pocket.

"Ryder." She tugged on his hand. "I'm not trying to tell you what to do, but maybe you should call your family?"

She was so pretty, she always looked so damn pretty. He studied her, enjoying the sight of his *wife*. He smiled, brushing a lock of her long golden hair from her shoulder. "Probably." The tip of her nose was red from the cold air. "But it'll take too long." He pulled his phone from his pocket, typed a short text and sent it.

"Ryder." She was clearly disappointed in him. Arms crossed, deep frown, hell, she was even tapping her foot.

He grinned. "Come on, Princess, let's eat." He held the door open for her.

"Morning, you two," Carl Stephens called out. "What's got you out and about on such a chilly morning?"

Ryder looked at Annabeth. She was blushing and he liked it. "Food," Ryder answered.

"What'll it be?" Carl asked. "The griddle's still going if you want some pancakes? Or French toast?"

"Pancakes, please." Annabeth nodded.

Ryder nodded, helping Annabeth shrug out of her coat. "Any chance of eggs and bacon or sausage, too?" He hung her coat over the back of her chair, then pulled the chair out for her.

"You bet. Help yourself to the coffee and all the trimmings. Lola's got all those flavor things and sweeteners, in case you're interested in making your coffee all fancy." Carl was hovering, watching every move he made.

Ryder's phone started vibrating again, bouncing off the metal button of his leather jacket. He saw Annabeth glance at him, her disapproving frown making him smile all the more. Something about his smile made her roll her eyes, and then he was laughing. And Carl, joined by Lola, looked back and forth between the two of them.

"Well, I'll be," Lola said, her eyes wide with excitement. "If that isn't a ring I see on your finger, Ryder Boone."

Carl bent forward, peering through the lower part of his glasses. "Is it?"

"Which means…" Lola turned to Annabeth, her hands clasped together and pressed to her chest.

Ryder watched the women, amused. His wife might not know it, but the flush on her cheeks told Lola the answer. He grinned as Annabeth held out her hand for the older woman's inspection.

Lola clapped her hands together. "I knew it! I just knew it. Your momma would be proud, damn proud to see who you married."

Ryder swallowed down the lump in his throat. He hoped so. He accepted Carl's enthusiastic handshake and Lola's hug before the rest of Pop's Bakery learned the news and jumped up to join in. Annabeth stood at his side, pink-cheeked and gracious and beautiful. Not as beautiful as she'd looked this morning, sleepy-eyed and smiling against the pillows. Memory gripped him, the silken skin of her cheek against his chest, the whisper of her breath. He'd woken up and bolted from the bed straight into a cold shower. And if he didn't think about something else real quick, everyone in Stonewall Crossing would know how much he wanted his wife.

"This is a surprise." Winnie Michaels was all wide-eyed assessment. "I never pegged you as the marrying sort, Ryder." Winnie smiled up at him. "Especially to someone as goody-goody as our Annabeth. Not your normal type—from what I hear anyway."

Ryder heard the edge in Winnie's voice. So did everyone else in the bakery. He knew some folks were going to give them a hard time—he expected it. But the slight tensing of Annabeth's shoulders, the way her smile dimmed, made him fiercely protective of her. "I'm lucky she'd have me." He took Annabeth's hand in his. It was ice-cold to the touch. He slid his arm around her shoulders, pulling her against his side.

Winnie's eyes narrowed. "Well, the timing is great. I mean, I'm sure she appreciates having someone to help out and support her while this whole job thing is going on." She smiled. "And, with you being a Boone and all, I guess that helps, too…" She looked back and forth between the two of them. "When are you two leaving for the honeymoon?"

Annabeth was ramrod stiff in his arms, her lips pressed flat. He needed to get her out of here, quick, before she let Winnie Michaels have a piece of her mind. While he would pay money to see his Annabeth put Winnie in her place, he suspected his wife would regret it. She worked too hard to be a model citizen in their small community. And having a catfight with one of her student's parents, however warranted, was not the sort of attention Annabeth needed right now. "Not for a while." Annabeth sounded cool and calm. He was impressed as hell.

"Lola, you think we could have that breakfast to go?" he asked.

"No honeymoon?" Winnie asked. "Isn't that bad luck? To not have a honeymoon?"

"We might not be going anywhere yet, but that doesn't mean there won't be a honeymoon." Ryder winked at Lola, but he made sure everyone heard him. There were more than a few snickers.

"You best hurry with their breakfast, Carl," Lola yelled

toward the kitchen, still giggling. "Don't want to keep these lovebirds waiting." She might be a gossip, but she had a good heart. She must know what he was up to, helping Annabeth into her coat, chattering away—and preventing Winnie from getting a word in edgewise.

"I imagine your family's tickled pink," Carl said, as he handed a large brown paper bag to Ryder.

"They don't think I deserve her." Ryder nodded, pulling his wallet from his back pocket.

"Nope." Carl waved his hand at him. "Consider it a little wedding present."

"Wonder how Greg's folks feel about it?" Winnie asked.

He drew in a deep breath. That was a question. A good question. He'd no interest in hurting Annabeth's relationship with the Uptons...but he might have already done that by getting her pregnant.

Annabeth's arm slid around his waist. "Judy and the Major love Ryder. He was the closest thing Greg had to a brother."

"You and Greg were two peas in a pod," Lola said with a nod.

"That's nice, then, keeping it in the family." Winnie smiled that mean, tight smile some women wear so well.

To his surprise, Annabeth laughed. "Oh, Winnie."

He had to give it to her, she knew how to make lemonade out of the bitterest of lemons. Even now, with Winnie prodding the grief-filled places in Annabeth's heart, she managed to laugh it off. What else could she do? He'd never been prouder.

He pulled her close, pressing a kiss to her forehead. "You ready to go, Mrs. Boone?"

Her huge hazel eyes turned on him, so full of warmth he could feel it. "I'm ready, Mr. Boone." Her smile grew. "And I'm starving."

She was talking about food, he knew it. Other than the night in his truck, she hadn't shown the slightest interest in him. But something about the look in her eyes and the husk in her voice sent his blood to boiling. He'd like nothing more than to take her home, feed her pancakes and spend the rest of the day—and maybe the night, too—in bed.

Chapter Seven

"What did you ever do to Winnie Michaels?" Ryder asked her as soon as they climbed into his truck.

She almost dropped the to-go cartons containing their breakfast. "What did *I* do?" She stared at him, ready to launch into all the things Winnie had done to her, when he started laughing. He knew about the teasing, the Annabeth Banana-breath. He'd been there.

"Teasing you." He was grinning ear to ear.

She sighed, sitting back in the seat, staring at his profile. A man shouldn't be that good-looking. His body was compact, lean and muscular—good for riding bulls. Her gaze drifted along his jean-encased thigh to his chest. She swallowed, remembering the feel of him all too well. Her inspection continued upward, his neck, his angled jaw. Full lips. Long, dark, lashes. Dirty-blond hair, cropped short. Chiseled bone structure and piercing pale blue eyes…that were looking at her right now. Her cheeks grew hot.

"Winnie's always been a…*charmer*," he said with a shake of his head.

"I wish I *had* done something. Then I could try to make amends." It was true. She didn't have many memories of Winnie that weren't "charming" in some way or the other. "How do people get that way?"

"What way?" He pulled the truck onto Main Street,

waving a greeting as they passed two locals sitting on a bench in front of the old courthouse.

"Twisted inside." She glanced at him. "Mean. She is. She's just...*mean*."

Ryder's gaze settled on her before he started laughing again.

"What?" she asked. His laugh was contagious. "Why are you laughing?"

Ryder rolled to stop at the stop sign and looked at her. "Because she was, without throwing a punch, picking a fight. And all you do is say she's *mean*?" He checked the street for traffic and headed to her house. "I can think of a long list of words to describe that woman. And mean is the mildest one of them."

She was laughing now, too.

"You're *amazing*, Annabeth," he murmured, cutting off her laugh immediately.

She glanced at him, curious. "Me?"

"Yeah, you. It might sound stupid, but I'm proud of you."

"You are?" she choked out.

"You didn't take the bait, even when it was being shoved down your throat." He glanced at her, looking a little uncomfortable. His next words were accompanied by a smile. "And... I like looking at you."

She rolled her eyes. "I can't decide if you're making fun of me or flattering me."

"I was trying to give you a compliment." He was smiling, but there was no trace of the usual teasing on his face.

"Well...thank you. I guess I could return the favor, but I'm sure you've had plenty of women go on about all of your praiseworthy assets. I wouldn't want to inflate your already healthy ego."

"*All*, huh?" He was grinning as he pulled his truck into her driveway next to Lady Blue.

"Exactly." She was laughing as she pushed open the car door.

And that's when the smell hit her. Nothing else smelled quite like it. Skunk.

"Don't see anything on the road." Ryder came around the front of the truck. "But it's somewhere close."

She nodded, her stomach instantly reacting to the fumes. "There goes my appetite." She shoved the bag with their breakfast into his hands and covered her nose, running to the porch steps.

And there, curled in a ball, was Tom. He was shivering, his pathetic mews instantly plucking at her heartstrings.

"How did you get out?" she said to the terrified kitten, stooping down to scoop the little fur ball into her arms. But the smell was so strong her eyes began to sting. That's when she noticed how matted and wet Tom's fur was. "Oh, no…"

"Up to no good, Tom?" Ryder was behind her. "I'll get him."

"I won't argue with you." She took a step back, her stomach roiling, nostrils burning and eyes watering fiercely. "I've got some tomato juice. And some tomato sauce, too, I think."

Ryder handed her back the bag containing their breakfast. "We'll need it—don't let him in the house. I'll get my gloves." Ryder made his way to his truck and popped open the lid of the large metal toolbox. "If you can squeeze by him, you might want to prep the bathroom."

Considering their strange beginnings, giving a kitten a tomato bath on her wedding day didn't seem all that out of place. She took a step toward the door and Tom leaped forward.

"Here's the thing," she said to the cat. "That mean old skunk is gone, so you're safe now. But I can't let you in the house smelling like that, Tom, sorry. The worst part's over."

Ryder returned, wearing a worn yellow raincoat and some well-used leather gloves. "He might disagree with you once the tomato juice bath starts." Ryder picked up the kitten, wrinkling his nose. "Whew-y. We'll wait here. You might want to change, too. Things are going to get loud and messy."

"What every bride wants to hear on her wedding day," she said, squeezing into the house.

Ryder's laughter followed her into the bedroom. She changed into a threadbare pale blue tank top and some yoga pants covered in paint splatters. Twisting her hair into a knot, she headed into the bathroom and removed all the linens and throw rugs. Less to get splattered with stink and tomato sauce. In the kitchen, she found four large cans of tomato juice—she could never resist a sale. She eyed a large jug of imported tomato sauce a student had given her for the holidays and grabbed it, too. Hopefully that would be enough. Tom was just a kitten, after all. A kitten with a lion-size stink.

She carried it all back to the bathroom, calling out, "Ready."

Tom was curled up against Ryder's chest, the power of the kitten's purrs surprising.

"Try making friends with a squirrel or a rabbit next time, will ya?" Ryder said, staring down into the adoring yellow eyes of the kitten he held. "They don't spray."

Annabeth's voice was muffled as she said, "Ready."

Tom's ears perked up and he turned toward the door, mewing once.

Ryder grinned. "You only think you wanna go in there." He pushed through the front door and headed straight into the bathroom.

Annabeth was there, practically naked in her skintight get up. He almost dropped the cat.

"Close the door." She waved him over, covering her nose with one hand. "Anything to contain the scent from the rest of the house."

He kicked the door shut behind him, sealing himself into the small room with a reeking cat and the most beautiful woman he'd ever met. And she did look beautiful, with her hair piled up in a messy knot and her huge hazel eyes peering over her hand. How could he be holding a skunk-coated cat and still want to kiss her? Hell, all he wanted to do was pull her against him and tug her hair free...

He had it bad. He needed to find a way to blow off some steam—and soon. "I got this," he growled.

Annabeth rolled her eyes, making the urge to kiss her that much stronger. "You can't hold him and wash him." She bent over the tub to pick up one of the cans of tomato juice. The sight of her rear made him groan. She popped up, holding a can. "Where do you want me?"

He stared at the ceiling, biting back a half dozen inappropriate suggestions before he bit out, "Bathtub."

She climbed in, scooting to the back of the tub, a can of tomato juice at the ready.

Ryder knelt on the floor beside the tub, holding Tom away from him. "You behave," he warned the cat.

"It's going to be okay, Tom." Annabeth's soothing tones caught the kitten's attention—and his. She smiled at the kitten then looked at Ryder. "You ready?"

He nodded, holding the kitten away from his body. He gripped Tom by the scruff of the neck, the other hand supporting the kitten's back legs.

Annabeth filled her hand with tomato juice and rubbed it into Tom's back.

And the kitten went crazy. Yowling, flying claws, growls, the little thing was in full panic.

Ryder kept a firm grip while Annabeth attempted to coat every inch of Tom. She rubbed juice in as thoroughly as the flailing limbs and claws would allow. Ryder watched, impressed with how unflinchingly she worked. Tomato juice spattered the front of her blue tank top and forehead, but she kept at it. She ignored the claw that scratched her forearm, working until every inch of Tom dripped tomato juice.

"You look like something from a horror movie." He laughed. "Both of you." It was true. Her shirt and pants and face had multiple tomato spatters—but it could almost be blood. Tom looked drowned and acted possessed.

Annabeth glared. "You should talk."

"Looks like we're all going to need a shower." He winked at her. "Wanna take one together?"

"Are you seriously hitting on me?" She kept rubbing tomato juice on Tom, and Tom kept yowling. "Now? While the cat is screaming bloody murder?"

He shrugged. "Bad timing?"

She laughed then, so surprised she slipped back, spilling tomato juice all over her shirt and pants. "Damn it!" She was still laughing.

"You okay?" Ryder shifted the kitten, making sure not to let go.

"Fine." She sat up, taking a deep breath and covering her nose with the back of her now dripping hand. "Yuck." She stared down at the pool of tomato juice in her lap.

"Time for a rinse?" he asked, turning on the warm water. He pulled the detachable showerhead free and offered it to her. "Ready?"

He pushed the pin in on the faucet and water sprayed from the handheld shower nozzle.

"Ryder," she squeaked. "I *wasn't* ready."

She was dripping wet, so was the ceiling. And the cat, and the small mirror over the sink.

"Ready now?" he asked, trying hard not to laugh.

She glared at him, shaking her hands at him and spattering him with tomato juice and water. "Yes," she hissed, aiming the nozzle at him.

"Hey, hey." He shook his head, holding the still-wailing Tom in front of him. "Aim for him."

"You've got a little something right there." She pointed at his chin.

"Let's get him taken care of first." He used his pickup voice, all low and coaxing. "Poor little guy could get a chill."

Annabeth rolled her eyes again, but immediately began rinsing Tom. A little baby shampoo and the cat was clean. He placed the kitten on the bathroom counter and started rubbing the squirming kitten brusquely with the one towel she'd left in the bathroom. "Hope you haven't lost your appetite?" he asked, looking back at her.

She stood, rinsing herself off with the showerhead. Her pale blue tank top was plastered to her, giving him a good view of her breasts. He'd imagined her, plenty of times, remembering the full weight of her curves beneath his hurried hands. But seeing her, knowing his fantasy didn't come close to the woman who was now his wife, did something to his insides.

"Well, hello there," Annabeth said to Tom, who was straddling the side of the tub, swatting at water drops. "You survived." The kitten mewed as she picked him up and sniffed him. Her nose wrinkled. "Better than it was, but…"

She was staring at him. He was standing there, gripping

the damn towel, staring right back. In a yellow raincoat. What the hell was the matter with him? "Need a towel?"

"Sure," she murmured, her cheeks turning red as she crossed her arms over her chest. "Thanks."

He opened the bathroom door and Tom skittered out. "You go on and shower," he murmured, pulling two towels from the built-in cabinet outside the bathroom and placing them on the counter. "I'll finish getting Tom dry and warm up our breakfast." He pulled the door shut and stood there, staring at the door.

Chapter Eight

Annabeth wiped the steam off the small bathroom mirror and looked at herself. Her breathing was uneven and her stomach twisted. Not because the lingering scent of skunk still hung in the air, but because of the look in Ryder's eyes. She didn't know what to think. Was she seeing what she wanted to see? Or was Ryder attracted to her? Could he actually see her, want her, as a woman?

She combed through her wet hair, tucked the towel tightly around her chest and opened the bathroom door. Tom was sitting right outside, his fur sticking up every which way.

He mewed at her, weaving his way between her ankles.

"Glad you don't hold a grudge," she spoke softly, smiling down at the kitten.

"Starting a load of laundry," Ryder called from the kitchen. "Wanna hand me your clothes and the towel?"

She peered around the corner to find Ryder pulling off his shirt and throwing it into the washing machine. The muscles in his back shifted and the waistband of his pants slipped low. His body was amazing, strong and capable and completely mind-blowing.

Swallowing, she hurried back into the bathroom, snatching her clothes and towels. Why was the sight of a shirtless Ryder getting her all flustered? She shot a look at her reflection. She'd been without a man for five years. No dating. No flirting. Nothing. Now she had someone who looked as though he'd stepped out of a muscle magazine stripping in her kitchen. Add in her raging pregnancy hormones and it made sense that she was a little disconcerted.

She strode back into the kitchen and shoved everything into the washing machine. But when she spun around, Ryder was staring at her.

She met his gaze. "Your turn." It shouldn't matter that she was wearing only a towel; she didn't have anything to put on after her shower. And she looked like a drowned rat.

The muscle in his jaw bulged. "My turn?"

"Shower." She swallowed. "It's all yours."

His attention wandered to her mouth. "You want to wash my back?" He reached for her, the pad of his thumb running along the curve of her neck.

She froze, fighting the slight shiver that ran along her spine. She would not press herself against the expansive wall of muscle that was his chest.

He took a step closer, one hand resting along her shoulder, the other cupped her cheek.

Her lungs emptied and her heart kicked into overdrive. They were half-naked in the kitchen. And she wanted him to kiss her more than anything.

But that couldn't happen. She couldn't let it happen. Kissing Ryder would only add to the confusion. They needed to talk—to come up with a plan. Now. A clear-headed plan without this newfound attraction muddying up the water. It was hard to push her longing aside, hard to resist the pull between them. But she had to. "I'm hungry," she blurted out.

He grinned. "In the microwave."

She turned, putting some much-needed space between them. "Thanks for starting the laundry."

"Got some clean clothes on the bike." He pointed toward the door. "Be back." He was out the front door before she could stop him. Out the front door, with his shirt off. If Mrs. Lavender saw him like that, everyone in Stonewall Crossing would hear about it. Then again, they were married now. It really shouldn't matter if he sat on the front porch in his boxers…

Married.

She was Ryder's wife.

She had to tell Cody.

She had to tell the Major and Judy, Greg's parents. She wanted to tell them in person—a phone call wouldn't do. They were the only parents she'd had since Flo's battle with dementia set in. Without them, she wouldn't be able to work the hours the principal position required. They looked forward to their weekend visits with their only grandson and loved it when she called for their help. She knew they needed Cody to keep Greg close to them. And, whether or not Ryder was in the picture, she had every intention of keeping that bond strong.

Ryder came back into the kitchen, pausing at the sight of her. Still wrapped in a towel standing in the kitchen. "Rethinking washing my back?" His pale blue eyes sparkled.

"No." She rolled her eyes. "I was thinking about Cody. And the Major and Judy."

Ryder's grin dimmed. "How are we going to tell them?"

"We?" His instant assumption that he'd be part of the conversation was a pleasant surprise.

He leaned against the door frame, his leather saddlebag gripped in one hand. It was impossible not to notice the play of muscles in his arm. "We."

"I was thinking about asking them for dinner tomorrow night? When they drop off Cody?" she suggested. "With Flo?"

He nodded. "Sounds good. You gonna eat?"

"I should probably get dressed first." She glanced down. "I don't know what's gotten into me."

"Cut yourself a break, Princess. You can't expect to come out of skunk duty looking dolled up."

She shook her head, suddenly exhausted. She yawned.

"I like the outfit." He pushed off the door frame, dropping a kiss on her temple before heading into the bathroom. "I just need to figure out how to get you out of it."

She shivered. He was teasing, she could hear it in his voice. "You're incredible."

"I've heard that before. Eat your pancakes. Then we'll take a nap."

A nap sounded too good to resist. "Then we talk."

He winked at her, pulling the door closed behind him.

She pressed the reheat button on the microwave and went to her bedroom, then slipped into a long cotton nightie and fuzzy socks. As she walked back into the kitchen, she heard Ryder humming in the shower. She was smiling as she sat down to her pancakes.

RYDER STARED DOWN at Annabeth. She was sound asleep, her long lashes resting against her cheeks. She'd kicked the quilts down to her knees and her thin nightgown did little to hide her stomach. His baby was in there.

After his shower and his late breakfast, he'd climbed into bed with her. He'd been working himself to death to wear himself out. He needed a nap as much as she did... and he couldn't pass up the chance to hold her. She'd been stiff, refusing to relax against him until she fell asleep. Once she'd drifted off, she had no problem wrapping herself around him. He closed his eyes, enjoying every second. The feel of her hand on his bare stomach. The whisper of her breath on his chest. The silk of her hair against his neck. Her scent, her little sounds and movements—she was driving him crazy.

He'd slipped from the bed and wandered through the kitchen. He folded the laundry, pulled on his clean clothes and poured himself a glass of orange juice. On the refrigerator door hung a brightly colored picture of a tree house. He smiled at Cody's creation. He knew the tree. It was a perfect tree house tree.

And he knew the house. The crudely drawn lilac-blue house in the picture was the perfect family house—a storybook house. Annabeth had always loved the Czinkovic place. When they were kids riding their bikes around town, she'd stop there. She'd had a plan, pointing out each window and explaining what each room would be if it was her house. Greg would nod, listening intently to every word she said. But Ryder hadn't understood her fascination with the place. Now he did. She'd wanted the family that lived there, not just the walls they lived in. She'd wanted everything he'd had and wanted to get away from.

He slipped out the back door of the house, careful not to disturb her. There was no fence, so he wasn't sure where Annabeth's yard ended and the Czinkovic house property line began. But a row of red-tipped petunias, two magnolia trees and several fruit trees made a sort of natural fence line. Cody's massive oak tree sat in the middle of the house's backyard. He stared up, seeing Cody's design in the sprawling limbs of the old tree.

He turned, assessing the house. It seemed to be in good shape, but he suspected it would need a thorough inspection. Some updates would be needed—wiring and plumbing. No signs of foundation concerns, but it would need lots of TLC.

He walked the property, sizing it up. Taking notes...

They would need a place to grow. Chances were his dad

would offer him property on the ranch to build, like he had with his brothers. But he'd always liked his space. Being in town, near Annabeth's work and Cody's school, made the most sense. Staying in Annabeth's teeny-tiny house didn't.

Once he'd written down the Realtor's name and number, he headed back to Annabeth's house. The yard needed raking, so he pulled open the shed and set to work. Most of her tools were in terrible shape. From the look of the lawn mower, he'd have to put more than elbow grease into it to get it running. He dug through the small shed until he found an old metal rake. Its handle was splintered and rough, but Annabeth had put a few layers of duct tape over the worst spots to keep using it. It made him smile, to see how resourceful she was. She knew how to take care of herself, without all the fancy bells and whistles. Not Annabeth. No, she made do with what she had—with a smile on her face. They may not have planned any of this, but he'd never had anything feel so right, so fast. He pulled on his work gloves and set to raking the leaves from the front yard.

Time and again, his gaze wandered to the empty house, imagining Cody sitting in the window, watching the birds. If he could give his family—something he never thought he'd have—a nice home, then he would.

Growing up, he'd never felt as though he fit anywhere, even at home. He wasn't as smart as his brothers. He'd struggled in school and had taken a lot of teasing for it. The more teasing he'd got, the angrier he'd become. The angrier he'd been, the more trouble he'd got into—striking out and earning a reputation that had made his father shake his head and his brothers lecture him whenever they'd had the chance. His mother had been his only defender. And then she'd died in a car accident coming to help him. And all he'd felt was anger.

When he was young, the rodeo had fit. Riding bulls had eased his restlessness. He'd loved the freedom, the fight, it gave him. It had kept him out of trouble, mostly. It didn't call to him the way it used to, but he still rode for the fun of it now and then.

But it was the vintage Packard his father had inherited from some long-lost aunt that had introduced Ryder to the real love of his life—cars. He could fix cars, build them from nothing or return them to their glory. He was a mechanic, working nine to five, and he was damn proud of that. Sure, he had a substantial share of the Boone fortune, but he'd never touched it. He'd wanted to make his own way—he'd needed to. Now he needed to take care of his family. He had a plan, one he was excited about.

When the yard was done and three large black bags were full of leaves, he crept back into the house. Staring down at her, at his baby, made him smile. "Annabeth?" he whispered.

Tom had been curled up against her side. The yellow-eyed glare he sent Ryder made him chuckle. Annabeth stirred a little, rolling onto her side and curling into a ball. The kitten climbed over her and curled up by her stomach.

"Princess?" he whispered again. "You're going to sleep the day away."

She rolled onto her back, blinking several times. "What time is it?"

"Almost five."

"Five?" She sat up, then grabbed her stomach and flopped back. "Remind me not to do that." Tom mewed, jostled by her sudden movements. "Sorry," she murmured to the kitten, scratching the little gray head.

He sat beside her on the bed. "Good nap?"

She nodded, yawning. "I feel great." He watched her

stretch, reaching over her head with her arms and extending her long legs with a satisfied squeal.

"Looks like it." He grinned, resisting the urge to touch her. Tom climbed into Ryder's lap, a vibrating ball of fur.

"What have you been up to?" She smiled a sleepy-smile at him.

Her smile made his heart thump. "A little yard work."

She frowned. "Ryder—"

His phone rang, interrupting what looked like another tirade about him helping out. He didn't even look at the phone as he answered. "Yeah?"

"We going to get something to eat before tonight?" DB's scratchy voice startled him.

"Tonight?" Ryder glanced at Annabeth, relaxed, propped up on the pillows, staring out the window.

"Rodeo? Tonight?" DB laughed. "You serious? You forgot?"

Ryder laughed. "Kinda had other things on my mind." Annabeth looked at him, her hazel eyes full of something he didn't understand. "I'm not gonna make it."

"What?" she asked, sitting up. "Don't change your plans."

"Call you back," Ryder said, hanging up the phone without waiting for a response from DB. "It's nothing, Princess."

"Tell me, then." She swung her legs over the side of the bed, putting her right beside him. She smelled like heaven. "If you committed to something, you need to follow through." He agreed, especially when it came to their marriage. If going tonight would help prove he was a man of his word, he would.

"Rodeo, in Smithville, tonight." He shrugged, smoothing a length of her long golden hair from her forehead. "It's nothing."

She covered his hand with hers. "I haven't been to the

rodeo in…a long time. Sounds like fun. We can have our talk tomorrow."

He laughed, turning his hand under hers and twining their fingers together. "Not exactly how I pictured tonight."

She stared at him. "You… How did you picture tonight?"

He swallowed. "You. Me. Here." He looked at the bed. "Right here."

Her cheeks turned an adorable red. "Ryder…stop." She blew out a long breath. "You…you don't…" She tried to pull her hand away but he wouldn't let go. "I think the rodeo is a much better idea—"

"I'm not so sure about that," he cut her off.

She rolled her eyes. "Well, I am." She tugged at her hand, sighing in frustration.

"Ouch," he murmured, reluctantly letting her hand slide from his.

"So, I'll find something to wear. And you can call whoever—" Annabeth stopped, staring at the phone. She closed her eyes, shaking her head. "Oh… Or would you rather I didn't go?"

"I'm only going 'cause you're making me, remember?" He stood, staring down at her. "So what's that about?"

She had a hard time holding his gaze. "I… I don't know much about your rodeo world…or if there's someone special. You know—a buckle bunny you've got a soft spot for?"

"Annabeth Boone." His voice was low. "After we go to the rodeo, would you go dancing with me? If memory serves, you loved to dance."

She hesitated, barely suppressing her excitement. "Are you sure?"

His hand slid through her hair, silk against his work-roughened fingers. "I'm sure. You're my wife and I'm fine with everyone knowing it." More than that, he wanted people to know it. He couldn't think of anything else he'd rather do—other than keeping her in bed all night.

"Then I'll get dressed," she said, pushing him out her bedroom door. "You could use another shower, cowboy."

"The bulls don't care," he argued.

"Well, I do," she sassed, her brows arching.

He knew that. And respected it. "Then I'll head to the apartment to get ready." He paused. "And I'll pack a bag?"

She blushed again, nodding, and so pretty he couldn't help himself. He leaned in, kissing her before she could argue. It was a soft kiss, a quick kiss, and not nearly enough to satisfy him.

Chapter Nine

Sitting in the stands, bundled in Ryder's thick Carhartt jacket, was easy. Watching Ryder flail around on the back of a bull that looked like evil with horns was not. She knew he rode bulls, and she'd seen him do it before. But they'd been young and death hadn't devastated her world. Now that it had, those eight seconds were the longest of her life. Reassuring herself over and over that Ryder was the most physically fit and capable man she'd ever known helped. At the same time, she knew he had no real control over the bull. All he could do was hold on.

When he jumped free, he dusted his brown Stetson on his thigh and sauntered to the gate. Annabeth jumped up, petrified. Apparently he didn't notice the thousand-pound bull circling the arena. But she did. It was only after he was safe behind the metal gate that she could swallow the lump of terror in her throat.

"You okay?" the woman beside her asked, bouncing her sleeping baby on her knee.

Annabeth realized she was standing up, making a spectacle out of herself. "Fine. Guess I got a little carried away." She started making her way from the stands. "Sorry," she murmured, careful not to step on anyone's purse, drink, or child.

When she was standing on the platform, the reality of

the day hit her. She was here, watching her husband, the father of the baby she carried, ride a bull. A bull. She was angry and relieved and so confused she could hardly see straight. Not that she had any right to be so mad—she'd been the one who'd forced him to ride. What was wrong with her? Why was she such a mess? Why did watching him tonight terrify her so? He was fine. Now she could relax. And when Ryder made his way onto the platform, making his way through handshakes and claps on the back, she couldn't decide whether to kiss him or leave.

His blue eyes found her and time seemed to stop. His cheeks were tinged with a ruddy flush. He moved with a sense of confidence. And the look on his face, the pure satisfaction, unlocked something deep inside her. He was so damn handsome, demanding her attention, her body's response, it worried her. Ryder would never be controlled—he wasn't built that way. It would be better if she kept him at a distance, smarter. But she didn't want to.

His expression shifted. His gaze swept her from her boot-clad feet to the headband she'd slipped on before they left. By the time he stood before her, the look in his eyes had her heart pounding a mile a minute. He stopped inches from her, the muscles of his jaw taut.

She wanted to wrap her arms around him, but said instead, "That was some ride."

He grinned, but the slightest furrow marred his brow. "You okay?"

"I'm a little wound up, I guess." That was putting it mildly. Never in her adult life had she fantasized about being kissed, passionately and publicly. But that's what she was thinking about. She wanted him to kiss her, to reassure her he was here, alive and well.

"Wound up?" he asked, leaning close. "You cold?"

She shook her head, then nodded. His arms slowly slid around her waist, triggering a shudder so strong she swayed into him. She stared at the pressed and starched blue shirt beneath her fingers, comforted by the feel of his heartbeat beneath her palm.

"Annabeth?" His voice was low and rough, drawing her gaze to his. "What's wrong?"

She couldn't put it into words. It had been so long since she'd felt like a woman, since she'd been aware of a man the way she was aware of him. It was exhilarating—and absolutely terrifying. "I guess I got scared." She tried to smile. "Been a while since I've seen you risking life and limb, you know?"

The furrow on his brow deepened. "Worried about me?"

She swallowed, the knot in her throat preventing her from answering. So she shrugged, staring at his chest again.

"Hey." He tipped her head back.

She hadn't meant to stare at his mouth, but she did. And her imagination went crazy.

"You keep that up and I'll kiss you." His whisper was husky, making her shudder again.

Her gaze met his, locking with those baby blues.

"You're beautiful." His gaze traveled over her face. "And, after some dancing, there will be some kissing."

She stepped away from him then, tugging the coat closed. "Then let's go dancing."

The look of surprise on his face had her laughing.

The rest of the night was like a dream. He took her to the only bar in Stonewall Crossing the locals frequented. She'd been there a handful of times, but had quickly learned that socializing with her students' parents could have negative side effects. Those times, she'd tended to hang by the pool tables, not the large retrofitted barn dance hall in the back. She loved dancing but since Greg died, she hadn't danced.

Ryder was the perfect gentleman, all charm and sass. He proudly introduced her to people she didn't know and reintroduced her as Mrs. Boone to those she did. After the initial shock, the response was pretty positive. And the shock was to be expected. He was who he was, with the reputation he had. To say settling down with the elementary school principal was a little out of character was a huge understatement.

"If he was going to settle down, there was no doubting who it'd be with." John Hardy, Ryder's boss at the garage, was all smiles.

Annabeth smiled back at him. "Are you saying he's been sweet on me?" She had to ask.

John laughed. "Oh, honey, that's an understatement."

Ryder's arm rested along the back of her chair, his fingers playing absently with her hair. He was talking to another man, Mario Rodriguez, one of the vet techs at the teaching hospital, totally unaware of their conversation.

"I never knew." Annabeth had a hard time believing Ryder cared about her in a romantic way.

"'Course not." John took a sip from his longneck. He leaned forward, lowering his voice. "Ryder took it hard when Greg died, real hard. Some days I could smell the liquor from the night before in his sweat. He didn't know which way was up. Then you called."

Annabeth leaned forward too, curious. "I called?"

He nodded. "You invited him to dinner."

She'd invited him to dinner several times…

"You lit into him for missing Cody's birthday." John shook his head.

Annabeth remembered then. Two years ago. "Cody was disappointed," she murmured. But that wasn't the whole truth. She'd been disappointed. Not seeing him there, among their friends and family, had felt wrong. If she dared admit it to herself, she'd been relying on Ryder even then.

When she looked at John, he was watching her. "He needed to know you missed him. That was all the permission he needed, I think."

"Permission?" she asked.

"To love you." John smiled.

To love her? Her heart twisted sharply. He loved her and Cody, she didn't doubt that. They were his family. But he didn't *love* love her. If he was dropping hints about getting her into bed—well, he was a man. And men rarely passed on the opportunity to jump into bed with a woman, according to every single female she knew. She was there. He was there. They were married. Why not hop into bed and make the most of the opportunity?

She looked at Ryder. How many nights had she woken up hot and bothered and tangled in twisted sheets? But could she live out those incredible dreams without falling in love with him? Because, if she gave in, she worried this time her heart would never recover.

The music changed, dropping into an easy rhythm, and Ryder took her hand. "Dancing time."

She clung to his hand and followed him onto the dance floor, a bundle of nerves. "Go easy on me. It's been a long time."

He spun her into him, sliding one arm around her waist. He dropped a soft kiss onto her lips. "Like riding a bike." His words tickled her ear. She was mind-numbingly aware of his hand on her lower back, of the intensity in his pale blue eyes. He pulled her closer, leaving no space between them. "Just hold on to me." And he started moving.

She couldn't think. She should be concentrating on not breaking his toes, but she couldn't break the hold of his gaze. Melting into him was her only option, so she did. He led, guiding her around the room with ease, as if there was no one else on the hardwood floor.

When the music ended, his hold didn't loosen.

She smiled, her nerves over dancing replaced by something entirely different.

The fiddler started again, the notes fast and short. Ryder grinned. "I've always wanted to do this with you." He took her hand and stepped away from her.

Always wanted?

It was the last thought she had before the steps demanded her attention. It took a while for them to get their speed up, but they figured it out. He pulled her in, turned them around then spun her up and under his arm before drawing her back into his chest. Faster and faster, they spun around the floor. The faster the music, the faster Ryder moved. Annabeth was downright breathless by the time the final note played.

"Damn, Princess." Ryder laughed, breathing hard.

"Not so bad yourself," she answered, laughing in turn.

"This next one is for Stonewall Crossing's own newlyweds, Annabeth and Ryder Boone," the band leader announced. "I, for one, am plum tickled to hear about this match."

The bright lights dimmed and the music slowed.

She stepped into Ryder, slipping her arm tight around his waist. From the look on his face, he seemed to approve. He kissed her forehead, took her hand in his and tucked her head against his chin. She rested her head on his chest, wrapped in his scent, the thundering of his heart and overwhelming happiness.

He was in love. He always had been—always would be. She was his wife, his Princess.

Holding her close, breathing her in, he knew he was where he needed to be. More important, he was where he wanted to be. He could only wish someday she'd feel the same.

His fingers slid through her long hair, stroking the fine strands between thumb and forefinger. If he angled his head just right, he could bury his nose in her hair and savor the citrus warmth of her scent. So he did, pressing her against him until her heartbeat echoed his.

The last call came two hours later, but they were still wrapped up on the dance floor. Spinning her like crazy, moving slow and holding her close, whatever it took to keep her in his arms. Maybe it was because everyone knew they were newlyweds, or it was clear he wasn't in the mood to share her, but no one tried to cut in.

"We just wanna thank y'all for a fantastic Saturday night. We'll be back the end of the month. Hope to see some of you then." The singer of the band tipped his hat back and took a bow.

"We'll have to come back," Annabeth said, clapping. "We could bring Cody. There's enough kids his age…" But her words cut short and her smile faded away. "Maybe." He watched her eyes sweep the room, no doubt evaluating the other kids that were there. Were they the kind of kids who would tease Cody? Or would he spend the night running around, having fun, smiling and laughing?

"Bet he'd enjoy it." Ryder took her hand as he led her off the dance floor. "We could bring Eli with us. The two of them seem to get along real well."

Annabeth's hazel gaze found his. "That might work."

Ryder held her white wool coat out. "I'm not just a pretty face, Princess."

She rolled her eyes, a bubble of laughter spilling from her full red lips. "Ryder—"

He slid her coat on and pressed a kiss to her cheek. "How are you feeling?"

"Exhausted." She turned, smiling up at him. "Thank you. I haven't had this much fun in years."

He shook his head. "That's a crime, Mrs. Boone."

She blushed, turning a very pretty color of pink. "It's just the way it is—"

"Was." He tugged on his leather jacket. "You ready?"

He didn't know why he felt nervous. Tonight had changed things. It wasn't about getting Annabeth into bed—not anymore. Maybe it was because he knew how he felt about her. He'd slept with plenty of women, but he'd never been in love with them. No, now it was about getting Annabeth—and keeping her. But he had no idea where to start—

"Penny for your thoughts?" Annabeth's question broke the silence on the short drive home.

"Nothing worth sharing." He was still coming to terms with the fact that he was in love with her.

"Work? Rodeo? Family?" she probed.

He glanced at her. "You light up when you dance. Must have missed it."

"After Greg died, it wasn't…a priority." She paused. "I don't know. Cody was a baby and Grandma Flo was just starting to get sick. And I was a single working parent." She started to laugh. "Dancing seemed…frivolous."

He looked at her then, a wave of admiration washing over him. She'd done so much on her own. "You're quite a woman."

She rolled her eyes. "I know, a real *Princess*."

He pulled into the driveway, put the truck in Park and looked at her. "You're stronger than most men I know."

The cab was dimly lit, but he knew her cheeks were tinged with color. She didn't know what to do with his compliments or how to respond.

"I'm waiting," she murmured, her fingers absentmindedly picking at the stitches on her wool coat.

"For?" But he knew. Normally he'd tack on some smart-ass comeback. Teasing had always been his way of keeping things from getting too serious. Now, serious was what he wanted.

She frowned.

"I mean it." He wanted to say something more, to tell her how special she was. But the words wouldn't come.

A furrow formed between her brows, but she didn't say anything. Instead, she turned her full attention to the bit of thread she'd worked loose on her coat. "We still haven't worked through what we're doing…how we're doing it."

"It?" he asked.

"The whole being-temporarily-married thing." She stumbled over the words.

Temporary. His lungs emptied, hard and fast. She wanted to make temporary plans. He wanted to make a real family. Now he needed to convince her of that.

"I imagine you have a few ideas." He leaned against his door. He stared out the front windshield of the truck, feeling like an idiot. Getting a woman into bed was a hell of a lot easier than getting into her heart. "Inside? Before all the heat's gone."

She nodded, sliding out of the truck without a word. He followed, fighting back his frustration and defeat.

Tom greeted them inside the door, mewing pathetically and winding between their legs.

"Guess he got lonely," Ryder said.

"Tom!" Annabeth froze in the kitchen door.

Ryder peeked over her shoulder. "He got lonely all right." Shredded bits of paper towel were spread all over the kitchen. Even the now-empty cardboard rolls were gnawed and tattered. "Come on, Mom, he got bored."

Annabeth glared at him. "Couldn't he read a book or something?"

"Bet he'd get a kick out of that." Ryder laughed, his mood lightening. "Rip it to pieces."

Annabeth shook her head, stooping to pick up the kitten that all but trembled from the power of his purring. "You are naughty." She held him close, her nose wrinkling up. "And you still stink." She giggled as he reached out with kneading paws. "Yes, yes, you're adorable." But she kept him at arm's length, her lips pressed tight.

Tom's purr echoed in the room.

"Tom, you be nice. She still loves you, but your...cologne might not agree with her delicate condition."

Annabeth sighed with exasperation—but she was smiling.

"The little guy can't help it, Princess. Cats are curious, it's in their nature." He took the kitten. "And he's a boy, so there's bound to be some mischief."

"Because mischief is part of the male's DNA?" she asked.

He nodded.

"You're making me rethink the need for a cat." She pulled the broom off the hook on the wall.

"Ah, come on now." Ryder put the squirming kitten down. "He's cute." He pushed off the door frame. "I'll clean up this time."

"Since this mess is your fault," she murmured.

He laughed.

"If you're sure you've got it under control, I'll get the chart." It was a question; he heard it.

"Discussing Option A?" He drew in a deep breath. "I think I can handle this."

She paused, her hazel eyes lingering on his face. "Thanks again—for tonight." She smiled. "I had a really nice time."

He didn't understand the look on her face, the way her gaze searched his. Now would be a good time to say something…sweet. But all the words he wanted to say lodged in his throat, making it impossible to say a thing. He cleared his throat, nodded and watched her walk away.

He dispensed with the paper towel while she busied herself in the living room. Once he was finished, he joined her there. Option A sucked. Living arrangements, time periods, divorce deadlines and custody arrangements… Not exactly what he was hoping for. Sure, she might have tried to show him that night, but he'd been too busy freaking out over getting her pregnant to think straight. Now… His stomach hurt as he read over it once, then again, before looking at her. "This is your plan?" he asked.

She nodded. "I don't want you to have to postpone the new job." She pointed at the chart but he didn't look away from her. "I figure the less time we live together, the easier it will be for Cody."

"I told you I wasn't going anywhere," he argued.

"And I told you I wasn't going to ruin this opportunity for you." She crossed her arms. "I won't do it. You've wanted to leave for…forever. Cody and I have a life here. I want to raise him here. I'll never keep the baby from you, ever. If you prefer, we'll work out set custody terms—alternating holidays and weekends." She shook her head. "It's just, this is home. And your family will want to be a part of this, too…"

"So they get to be a part of his future, but I get holidays and weekends?"

"If you want—"

"You think it's that easy? That no one's going to care that I up and left you while you were pregnant?" he interrupted, his frustration mounting.

She frowned. "Then why did you marry me?"

He sighed, his hands on his hips. "I told you why." *Stubborn woman.*

"To do the right thing? So that's it? You're going to *settle*? Life in a town you hate. Working at a place that will always be your second choice. Married to a woman you don't love. And saddled with a baby you never wanted? Every day will be consumed with regret and resentment. That's no way to live—"

"And you married me because—?" he countered.

"I thought… I don't know. I panicked." She stumbled over her words. "It was temporary. A way for us both to *survive*."

He stared at the poster. *She still doesn't trust me.* "So we live together, but apart." He flicked the sticky note that read No Sexual Relations. "Until May tenth?" He looked at her. "Why May tenth?"

"It's after the school board meeting. And it's a school holiday, a long weekend. I can send Cody to the Uptons and you can go to Dallas, if they'll let you wait?" she asked. "It'll be easier for you to move out…" She grabbed his arm. "*I'm* going to take the fall for this. I will make this okay."

"No one will believe it, Princess." He smiled, covering her hand with his. He tried to keep the sneer off his face. "I'm good at being the bad guy."

She shook her head. "I'll tell everyone I still love Greg. No one can argue with that." She paused. "We're friends, Ryder, good friends. And, together, we'll be good parents."

Her words cut like a knife. "If this is what you want, I'll try." But not for Option A. No, he'd try his hardest to win her heart.

He stared at the chart again, drawing in a deep breath. The sooner Option A was on a burn pile or shredded in the trash, the happier he'd be. Nothing got in his way when he set his mind to it. And he'd set his mind on keeping his wife.

Chapter Ten

"Mom!" Cody climbed out of her father-in-law's car and came barreling across the yard to her waiting arms.

Annabeth swallowed the butterflies and caught Cody in a big hug. "Missed you."

"I missed you, too. How is Tom?" he asked. "Hey, R-Ryder," he added, grinning at Ryder.

"Tom's a little smelly," she said, wrinkling her nose. "Ryder and I really tried to clean him up, but I think skunk spray must have some glue in it."

"Skunk?" Cody frowned. "How'd he get o-o-outside?"

"He must have slipped out." Annabeth shrugged. "I think it turned out for the best, though. He doesn't want out anymore."

"You should have seen your mom, Cody. She was covered in tomato juice, from head to toe." Ryder laughed.

"Get p-pictures?" Cody asked.

"No." Annabeth sighed. "He acted like a true gentleman—until he mentioned it now."

"I would've liked to see that myself." Her father-in-law laughed. "I've rarely seen her with a hair out of place."

"Good to see you, Major." Annabeth kissed the older man on the cheek. "Good weekend?"

"With Cody around? Of course." He grinned at his

grandson. "Nice to see you, Ryder. You're looking fit." He shook Ryder's hand.

Annabeth watched, nervous over the Major and Judy's reaction to her marriage. They'd always loved Ryder. And, after last night, she was truly worried about making him the villain when she knew he was the hero.

Ryder nodded. "You, too, sir."

"It's been a long time." Judy hugged her, then Ryder. She looked back and forth between the two of them, smiling. "Seeing you together… I almost expect Greg to walk out that door…any minute." Her voice trembled a little, the smile on her face dimming.

The Major was surprisingly demonstrative with his wife, something Annabeth had always loved about him. So it was no surprise to see him wrap a supporting arm around his wife's waist.

"We all miss him," Ryder said.

She looked at him, taking in the very real grief on his face. Of course he missed Greg. He'd been his best friend, his brother, his sounding board about life. They had that in common, missing Greg. She smiled at Ryder, clasping her hands so she wouldn't be tempted to reach for him.

It was unexpected, how easy it was to fall into a routine with this man. He'd tried to sleep in Cody's bed last night, but it was too small. And the couch was hard as rocks. So, for the second night in a row, she'd slept wrapped in his arms. And she'd actually slept, without dreams or interruption, just deep, invigorating, peaceful sleep. Waking up was another matter. She'd never woken up so responsive—and hungry—for another's touch.

Not that she needed to be thinking about it now, face-to-face with Greg's parents.

"Come meet Tom!" Cody waved his grandparents into the house excitedly.

"Can't wait to meet him. I feel like I know him already." Judy smiled at her as she followed Cody down the hall to his bedroom.

"Want a drink?" Annabeth asked her father-in-law.

"Thank you, Annabeth." The Major sat. "What have you been up to, Ryder? Judy and I saw you last season when you came through at the Marble Falls rodeo. She about came unglued when you got carried out of the arena after that bull turned his head into your shoulder." The Major shook his head. "Damn physical work."

"Lucky nothing broke that time," Ryder admitted, glancing quickly at her. "Been spending a lot more time working at John Hardy's garage, less time on a bull."

"That's good to hear." The Major sounded genuinely relieved.

Ryder smiled. "A fella's luck can only last so long."

She didn't want to think about that. "Day jobs aren't too bad," she interrupted. "As long as you like what you do." She loved her job—headaches and all.

"How's the school?" The Major accepted the glass of ice tea she offered him. "Thank you."

She wrinkled her nose. "I'm looking forward to summer."

"Cody was telling us you're worrying over your job?"

She blinked. "He was?" So much for trying to shield Cody from stress. She frowned, quickly explaining things. "There's no point in worrying over it, I know that. Grandma Flo would tell me to keep my chin up and my big-girl britches on."

Major and Ryder laughed.

"Good advice, I suppose," the Major said with a chuckle.

"You'll keep the job." Ryder was so confident.

She shrugged, unable to ignore the pleasure his words

stirred. His belief in her meant more than it should. "We'll see."

Judy joined them then, a strange look on her face. "I know this is none of my business…" Judy glanced over her shoulder then whispered, "Is there a man in your life, Annabeth?"

"Why on earth would you ask her that, Judy?" The Major looked stunned.

"There's a man's shirt on her bed," Judy said. "And a pair of boots peeking out from under her bed. Not that I was snooping… The door was open…"

All eyes were on her. And, from the heat in her face, she knew she was turning very red. The Major scowled, Judy tried for a smile and Ryder looked ready to laugh.

"Do we know him?" the Major asked.

She opened her mouth, but Judy interrupted. "How does Cody feel about him?"

She took Judy's hand in hers, knowing her mother-in-law worried about anything that would threaten the bond she had with her only grandchild. "Cody loves him, very much." Which was absolutely true.

Judy nodded, visibly relieved. "Well, then, I like him already."

"What's his full name?" the Major asked. "And his birthday."

"Major, you are not going to run a background check on him," Judy chastised.

Ryder chuckled then, earning the full weight of the Major's scowl and a disapproving shake of Judy's head. He held up his hands in surrender. "No need." He took a deep breath. "I'm the no-good man in her life. We got married this weekend."

The kitchen was absolutely silent.

Ryder glanced back and forth between Judy and the

Major, all teasing gone. "I promise you both, I'll do right by her, by Cody, and Greg, too."

Pressure squeezed her chest, momentarily knocking the breath out of her. Whether it was the look on Ryder's face or the weight of his words, she couldn't be sure. When he reached out to her, she took his hand and let him draw her into his side.

Judy burst into tears. "I'm so happy." She sniffed, taking the handkerchief her husband offered her. "I prayed, you have no idea how hard I prayed."

The Major took Ryder's hand, pumping it heartily. "Guess I can't say I'm completely surprised, but it would've been nice to have been at the wedding."

"We just went to the justice of the peace. I didn't want anything fancy this time around. But Renata is planning quite a party, and I hope you'll come," she said to soothe the Major. "It would mean a lot…if you're free."

"Of course we'll come." Judy was still dabbing at her tears. "Cody will be over the moon."

Annabeth nodded.

"'Bout what?" Cody carried Tom into the room.

"Your mom has some big news," the Major spoke. "Your Grandma and I are going to head out. But we'll see you later this week?"

Annabeth frowned. "You're not staying for dinner?"

"Not tonight." The Major shook his head. "You have a nice dinner, just your little family—this time."

"Once we know what Renata's planned, we'll let you know," Ryder agreed.

After another ten minutes of goodbye hugs and happy tears, Annabeth flopped onto the couch and patted the cushion next to her.

Cody sat, looking up at her with round eyes. "What's wrong?"

"Nothing," she reassured, taking his hands in hers. "Nothing at all. I have to tell you something and it just occurred to me you might be mad about it."

"Why?" Cody asked.

Annabeth glanced at Ryder, who shrugged. "Well, I probably should have talked to you about it—"

"I should have asked you first," Ryder jumped in, sitting beside Cody.

"Asked?"

"If I could marry your mom." Ryder's words were so calm it took a minute for Annabeth to realize what he'd said.

"M-marry Mom?" Cody looked back and forth between the two of them. "You want *me* to say if it's o-okay?"

Ryder nodded.

Cody stood up and faced them. He crossed his little arms over his chest, tapping his left pointer finger on his chin. Annabeth couldn't help but smile, glancing Ryder's way to gauge his reaction. Ryder wasn't smiling. If anything, he looked worried.

"Will you help her?" Cody asked. "So she d-doesn't have to w-worry 'bout money?"

She leaned forward, resting her elbows on her knees. "Cody—"

"Yes." Ryder nodded.

"She works so hard because she *has* to." Cody glanced at her, almost apologetically. "So she can take care of me and G-Grandma Flo. But you can h-help with all that."

"I will." Ryder nodded. "But I'll tell you, Cody, I've never known your mom to do something she didn't want to do."

She sat back, listening to them. Apparently her son knew everything. Relying on Ryder to "fix it" didn't sit well with her, though. She couldn't afford to trust anyone else. It was a risk, relying on him, for her or her children's future.

"I guess." Cody shrugged.

"Are you two done? Not that either of you asked, but I love my job." She sighed. "I feel important—and I like being able to provide for you." She stood, ruffling Cody's hair as she headed into the kitchen. "Anyone want some lemonade?"

"No, th-thank you," Cody answered.

She glanced back, waiting for Ryder's response. But that's when she saw it. Ryder loved Cody. There was no denying the tenderness on his face, the look of a father. It took her breath away.

Ryder's pale blue eyes settled on her. "I'm good."

She nodded, hurrying into the kitchen. Her heart was pounding. Just when she thought she knew how to handle Ryder Boone, he threw her a curveball. It was one thing to be a gentleman, to step up when he should. It was another thing altogether to let another man's child into his heart—to love unconditionally.

She took a sip of lemonade and her stomach growled. She glanced down, placing both hands over the slight swell of her belly. She should eat something.

"Ma?" Cody asked, standing in the doorway with Ryder. "You o-okay?" Her son was looking at her, but Ryder was staring at her stomach. Ryder's hand rested on Cody's shoulder.

"I'm good." She smoothed her shirt. "What did you two decide?"

"Yes. Of c-course." Cody looked up at Ryder. "I'm glad he's g-gonna be my dad."

Ryder nodded, squeezing his shoulder.

Her heart ached at her son's easy declaration. She looked at Ryder, then Cody, and blew out a slow breath. Maybe her plan was a huge mistake. One that would hurt everyone. Not that there was anything she could do about it now. She nodded, forcing herself to smile. "Now that that's decided, how about you tell me what we're making for dinner with Grandma Flo," she said, opening the refrigerator and looking inside. There wasn't much to choose from. Grocery shopping hadn't been a priority this weekend.

"Waffles?" Cody asked, staring into the fridge.

She smiled down at him. How many nights had she fed him waffles recently? For the evenings when she was too tired to cook a real meal, waffles had become a staple. Not that Cody complained. He didn't complain about anything.

"Waffles sound good," Ryder agreed. "You're in luck. I can actually cook waffles." He moved the milk jug. "And bacon. And eggs."

"You think Grandma Flo will approve?" she asked.

"She wants to be with us, Ma." Cody smiled. "I don't think she cares 'bout the food."

That was one long sentence. A long sentence without a single stutter. She glanced at Ryder, saw the smile he was wearing and knew he'd caught it, too.

"What time do we need to get her?" Ryder asked.

Annabeth glanced at the clock. It was four thirty. On a Sunday. The weekend had gone too fast. "Now."

"Cody and I'll go," Ryder offered. "In case there's something you need to do to get ready for the week."

"Yeah, Ma, you chill," Cody piped up.

"Chill?" She burst out laughing.

Cody nodded, grinning.

"I'll get some laundry going and then I'll chill." She ruffled his hair.

Cody stood on tiptoe, kissing her cheek. Ryder leaned forward, adding his kiss to her cheek. Cody's grin grew bigger.

She rolled her eyes, making Ryder wiggle his eyebrows at her. "We'll be back shortly, Mrs. Boone."

Cody giggled, all but bouncing out the front door.

RYDER WAS EXHAUSTED and it was only Tuesday. The past few weeks had been some of the best of his life. He had a family, one he was proud of. There were lots of smiles around the dinner table, easy conversation and active interest in each other.

Last night had been…different and frustrating. A lot of his frustration was his own fault. He knew he should sleep on her lumpy couch at night, but he couldn't do it. Lying next to Annabeth, feeling her against him, was something he looked forward to all day. But last night she'd been restless. She'd whispered Greg's name in her sleep, almost a plea. Guilt consumed him, followed by anger. Not at her, or Greg, but himself. Even now, she'd pick Greg over him. Because she could rely on Greg—something she still couldn't do with him. As misplaced as it was, he was jealous. Of Greg. His dead best friend. What was wrong with him?

He'd stared up at the ceiling, frustration coursing through him. He'd been ready to slip out of bed and the house when she whimpered.

He'd rolled onto his side. Moonlight had spilled through her lace curtains, making it easy to see her erratic breathing, the rapid-fire shift of emotions on her face. Whatever she'd been dreaming about, it wasn't good. He'd pulled her close—to soothe her. And, maybe, himself.

Then her hands had slid down his chest, edging toward the waist of his boxers and making him ache. When he'd tried to disentangle her, she'd kissed him. It had taken every ounce of control not to respond. He'd wanted to— he'd been about to burst. But she'd been asleep. Instead, he'd wrapped her in his arms and tucked her against his chest.

She'd sighed, turning her face into his chest.

He might have controlled his body, but his mind had had other ideas. Every time he would doze off, Annabeth would be there—wanting him as much as he wanted her. He'd wake with a start, on edge and breathing hard. Over and over, all night long. He hadn't gotten much sleep.

He drove by the house, but there was no one there so he headed to the elementary school. Lady Blue was one of the only cars in the parking lot.

He parked and headed inside.

She didn't see him, lost in the pile of files stacked high on her desk. Her cheek rested on one fisted hand. The other tapped a pen against whatever she was reading. She seemed just as tense and edgy as he was.

But then she dropped the pen and leaned back in her chair, covering her stomach with her hands.

"You okay?" he asked.

She almost jumped out of her chair. "You scared me to death."

"Sorry." He came into the office, sitting on the corner of her desk. "Wondering if you were done for the day. If not, I could take Cody home."

She glanced at her computer screen. "Dammit."

He laughed.

"Is it really six o'clock?" she grumbled, standing and stretching.

"Long day?" he asked, noting the circles under her eyes.

"You could say that." She looked at him, frowning.

"What'd I do now?" he asked, longing to pull her against him for a nice long hug.

"This." Her voice was pinched—he'd never heard her sound like that. He took the narrow coil of paper she handed him but stared at her. Something was wrong. Very wrong. "You okay?"

"Look." She all but snapped the word at him.

So he did. The images in the small squares were black-and-white, too grainy to tell what they were of. "Am I supposed to know what this is?" He stared at the images. Her sigh was so exasperated that he forgot all about the paper he was holding. "What's wrong, Annabeth? Talk to me."

"That's… Those are the babies." Her voice was tight and high-pitched.

He inspected the paper again. "Where?"

She shook her head, leaning against him to point out a white dot. "There…and there." Her finger tapped another dot.

He froze. "Two?"

"Yes, two." There was that strange, squeaky voice again. "Two."

He dropped the paper on the desk and wrapped both arms around her. He pulled her close, offering her comfort he knew she needed. "Hey now," he spoke softly. "It's going to be okay, Annabeth."

She was rigid in his arms.

"Are you okay?" He kept his tone low, soothing. "What did the doctor say?" Why hadn't he known she had a doctor's appointment? He'd have gone with her. He wanted to be a part of this. But, from the way she was acting, now wasn't the time to have that conversation.

"I'm fine. Too skinny, but fine." Her words were mumbled.

She felt just right to him. "We can fix that." His hands kept a steady rhythm, rubbing up and down her back. "Anything else?"

"Besides the fact that there's two of them?" She wasn't squeaking anymore, but she was a long way from relaxed.

He pulled back. "Annabeth."

She looked at him, her hazel eyes sparkling with unshed tears.

He swallowed, fighting the need to run far away from the depths of emotion he saw there. This was Annabeth and she needed him. Right now. He wasn't going anywhere. "Let's go get something to eat, get Cody in bed and I'll give you a foot rub."

Her chin quivered. She took a deep breath and pressed her lips together.

"Everything's going to be okay," he repeated, for both of them. He tilted her head back, pressing a soft kiss to her lips.

She melted against him then, twining her arms around his neck and burying her face against his neck. "And a bubble bath?" she murmured softly.

"Whatever you want, Princess," he promised.

He didn't move, enjoying how they fit together.

"Anything?" she asked.

He swallowed, wishing the memory of his dream didn't immediately spring to mind. He nodded.

"Even if it's ice cream?"

He smiled. "For dinner?"

"Dessert?" She looked up at him, the first glimpse of a smile on her face.

"Definitely." He kissed her again, unable to resist.

And she kissed him back. Soft, sweet, clinging just enough to force his pulse into a rapid beat.

"I like kissing you, Mrs. Boone," he murmured against her lips. "Even if it's not part of Option A."

Her expression changed, uncertain and flustered. Her gaze traveled over his face, that small crease forming between her brows. He reached up, smoothing the crease before cupping her cheek in his palm. Her skin was satin in his rough palm.

"I like ice cream." Her voice wavered.

He shook his head, taking her hand in his. "Let's get out of here then go get my kids and my woman some food."

She paled, tugging free of his hold to turn off her computer. "Give me five minutes?"

"Sure." He shoved his hands into his pockets. "Where's Cody?"

"In the gym. Now that he's figured out how to dribble, he can't get enough of it." She didn't look at him as she tidied the stacks on her desk.

"I'll go get him." Women were emotional when they were expecting, or so he'd heard. If she was all over the place right now, he needed to be as calm as possible. Even though he wasn't.

Twins. One baby was challenging. But twins? He grinned.

He headed for the gym, remembering all of the concerts and events he'd attended for Hunter's son, Eli. It only now occurred to him that he was going to be spending a lot of time here. Between Annabeth, Cody and the babies... Well, he might as well get comfortable with the place.

Chapter Eleven

"You're the luckiest woman on the planet." Janet Garza pulled her copies off the copy machine. "Seriously, you have no idea how jealous Abigail, Lori and Maricella are. When he came up here to pick up Cody... The things they're saying about what they want to do to your husband." She fanned herself with a bundle of papers. "I guess it's okay, as long as none of the kids overhear. We'd be corrupting minors." She laughed.

Annabeth smiled, pulling the ink refill cartridge from the supply cabinet before locking it. "I don't think I want to know."

"Probably not. Not that I'd peg you as the jealous overprotective type, but I wouldn't want you to harbor any negative thoughts about coworkers." Janet winked.

She didn't think she was normally very jealous or overprotective, but that's exactly the way she was feeling. "Which is why you're telling me this?" Annabeth shook her head. She and Janet had taught the fourth grade together for three years. Annabeth respected her as a teacher and liked her as a person, but Janet was fond of telling a good tale.

Janet shrugged. "I didn't say anything. Not really." She pressed some more buttons, then turned. "Oh, but I didn't get to tell you about Winnie."

Annabeth held up her hand. The last thing she wanted was information on Winnie Michaels—unless she was moving. "I'll take a pass on that one, Janet." She glanced at the clock. "The decorating committee's in the gym to set up for the spring concert tomorrow." She waved at Janet, dropped off the ink cartridge in her office and headed to the gym—also their cafeteria. It was lunchtime, so the noise level was a low roar. The old-fashioned street sign in the corner reminded the students to keep their chatter at yellow or below. It was yellow but, to Annabeth's ears, it was nearing the red light.

A few moms and one father stood on the small stage, several boxes stacked in front of them. Annabeth knew them all by name—they were the go-to parents for every event throughout the year.

"Good to see you, Holly, Jim, Irene and Carol." She shook each of their hands. "What's the plan for tomorrow night?"

"Well, hello, Mrs. *Boone*." Carol nudged her with her elbow. "How have you been? Anything exciting happen recently?"

"Oh, that's right, I think I heard something?" Holly joined in.

Jim just shook his head, chuckling.

"I'm sure it's just gossip," Irene added, grinning. "Right, Mrs. *Boone*?"

Annabeth resisted the urge to roll her eyes. "You mean me getting married?" she asked. "Yes, it's true."

"Nothing wrong with marrying your best friend," Jim mumbled. "Solid start."

Annabeth nodded. It was a good reason for getting married. And a much better reason than Ryder getting her knocked up. With twins. *Twins.* She swallowed, still digesting yesterday's news. "Thank you, Jim."

She laughed through the chorus of congratulations and hugs, wanting to talk about anything but her marriage. Her constant state of frustration, her irritability—she didn't know why she couldn't shake it. All she wanted was some time to herself, to have a long cry…or to take her husband to bed and do all the things she'd been dreaming about. She couldn't take any more surprises—she needed continuity and reliability. Things she knew Ryder couldn't offer her.

Carol was talking. "…and Holly found a bunch of flower garlands and lantern lights on clearance last year—"

"Couldn't get the box in my car but I'll bring it up after school," Holly offered.

"Besides the ladder, what will you need?" Annabeth asked.

"Able bodies," Jim interjected. "Maybe you can ask that new husband of yours to come lend a hand."

"I'll ask him," she agreed reluctantly. She didn't want Ryder to become a fixture here, too. It was bad enough that he'd slipped so easily into her life. He was everywhere, a reminder of everything she wanted but was destined to lose again. The sound of his voice eased her. His scent both calmed and excited her. She couldn't wait for bedtime so his arms would cradle her against him all night long. It was ridiculous. She was *acting* ridiculous.

And then there was Cody. He was crazy about Ryder and he had no problem showing it. Ryder seemed just as enamored with his stepson, holding his hand, answering the million questions Cody would ask about cars and the rodeo at the dinner table. But what would happen when Ryder left? Cody would be crushed.

And it would be her fault. Since he'd been born, she'd invested so much time and energy into making sure Cody was taken care of. Now one stupid mistake could break his little heart.

"Can we send out this reminder note?" Irene asked, holding out a paper to her.

Annabeth scanned the note, nodding. "Sure. It'll go home this afternoon."

"I think that's everything." Holly shrugged. "I'll bring the box up after school."

"And I'll try to get some extra hands to help out," Annabeth assured them, her attention wandering around the cafeteria. Kindergarten and first grade were eating now, requiring all hands on deck.

"Two big nights in one week," Irene spoke up. "Hope you don't have to work too late this week, or you'll be wiped out before your party this weekend."

This weekend. The wedding party. Right.

Renata had been as good as her word. It seemed like all of Stonewall Crossing was coming to the Lodge on the Boone Ranch Friday night for her and Ryder's wedding party. It was Wednesday and she was already dreading it. As if her pregnancy nausea wasn't bad enough, now her stress was getting out of control.

"Isn't the school board meeting this week?" Jim asked.

"No," Annabeth assured him. "Not yet." She smiled. She had a few more weeks to worry over a job she couldn't afford to lose—especially not with twins on the way. Annabeth turned right as a piece of fruit cocktail flew across the cafeteria. "That's my call."

"Go get 'em," Carol called after her.

Annabeth made her way to the kindergarten table. She arched her discipline eyebrow and waited. At this age, all it took was a stern face before the culprit came clean. Sure enough, Hugh burst into apologetic tears.

"He didn't mean to, Ms. Upton," another classmate, Franz, sounded off. "It...slipped."

Annabeth refused to smile. "It slipped?"

Hugh, still crying, looked at Franz in sheer confusion. But Franz refused to budge. "Off his spoon."

Annabeth narrowed her eyes. "Will any more fruit be slipping off your spoon?"

Every head at the table shook simultaneously, making it even harder to maintain her disciplinarian stance. "I hope not."

She walked around the cafeteria, trying to ignore the way her stomach rebelled. She couldn't throw up; there was nothing left in her stomach. And she didn't want to go back to her office. Sitting only made it worse. Being up and walking around made her stomach bearable—most of the time.

"My turn," Ken Branson said as he approached her.

"It's fine." She smiled.

"No, really, I'll take it from here," he assured, patting her shoulder.

"Okay." She headed back to the main office, confused by Ken's willingness to stay in the cafeteria. He hated cafeteria duty. He hated pretty much anything to do with actual kid interaction at this point. Once she walked into the main office, his attitude made sense. Kevin Michaels sat, his arms crossed, scowling. When he was angry, there was no doubting he was Winnie's son.

"Is Kevin here to see me, Ms. Barnes?" Annabeth asked the school secretary.

"Yes, ma'am." Mrs. Barnes nodded, looking apologetic.

"Do you have a teacher's referral for me?" she asked Kevin.

He thrust the paper at her but wouldn't look at her.

Annabeth scanned over the notes the teacher had made. "Looks like we need to have a talk in my office."

Kevin looked at her then, so angry his jaw was tight. "Gonna call my mom?"

Annabeth read over the referral again. *Maybe not.* "I'd like to hear your side of things first."

Apparently that wasn't the answer he was expecting. His eyebrows rose and his jaw relaxed a little. He stood, leading the way to her office. Once he was seated in one of the two chairs facing her desk, she sat in the other.

"Why did you threaten to punch Billy in the face?" she asked.

Kevin frowned, crossing his arms over his chest.

"You and Billy are friends," she prodded gently.

Kevin glanced at her, then at the picture of Cody on her desk. He frowned. "He said something."

Annabeth's stomach chose that moment to make a sci-fi movie sound.

Kevin laughed, too surprised not to. "You okay, Ms. Upton?" He looked at Cody's picture again. "Mrs. Boone."

"Haven't had time for lunch." She tried to redirect him. "What did Billy say? *Exactly?*"

Kevin sighed. "He was talking about my mom."

Annabeth didn't say a word. Kevin Michaels might be a pain in her rear, but he loved his mother. "Can you tell me what he said?" Her stomach clenched, so she shifted in her chair.

Kevin shook his head.

"How about you write it down." She shifted again, trying to find a comfortable position.

Kevin didn't react.

Annabeth stood, rifling through her drawer for a packet of crackers. "I can call Billy in," she offered.

Kevin shook his head fiercely.

"Kevin, if you're not willing to tell me what happened, then I don't have a choice." She broke off a tiny piece of cracker and chewed it slowly. She was out of ginger ale, so this would have to do. "This is your chance."

"He said my mom was a piece of trash and nobody likes her." Kevin's voice hitched. "And he called me a liar."

Annabeth's heart sank. Nobody liked to hear someone talk about their family that way. "What happened before that?"

Kevin leaned forward, his face turning red. "You mean did I do something?" he yelled.

"I need the whole picture, Kevin." Annabeth stayed calm. "Billy had no right to say those things, but it will help me decide how to handle it if I know everything."

Kevin sat back, crossing his arms over his chest again.

She sat at her desk, turning her attention to the paperwork spread out across her desk. If he wasn't ready to talk, she'd give him some time to think things through. Kevin was very good at pressing buttons. Something more had happened to make Billy fight back.

"I said Ryder Boone had asked my mom to marry him and she turned him down." Kevin's words were thick, as though he was having to work to get them out.

Once they were, Annabeth wasn't sure what to do about it. Billy's parents worked on the Boone Ranch—his mother was a cook at the Lodge and his father a gamekeeper. So Billy, like so many in Stonewall Crossing, were protective of the Boone family.

"Is that true?" Annabeth asked. She knew it wasn't.

Kevin scowled at her.

"Kevin—"

"Why wouldn't it be?" Kevin snapped. "My mom's way prettier than you are." Kevin's voice rose as he kept talking. "And I don't talk funny like Cody does. He could love us, if he wanted to. Why wouldn't he want us instead of you?" He sniffed, on the verge of tears. "Why not?"

He broke her heart. She couldn't be mad at him, even if the words were hard to hear. Every boy wanted a father, someone to love their mother. By defending the Boones, Billy had hit on Kevin's biggest weakness.

Movement in the doorway caught her eye. Bryan Goebel stood there, hovering just outside, probably concerned over Kevin's noise level. She gave the slightest shake of her head. He stepped back, but his shadow lingered on her office floor.

"People can't choose who they love, Kevin." She spoke softly. "It's hard, isn't it, living without a dad?"

"You don't know." Kevin frowned at her. "Your life is perfect."

She folded her hands on her desk, swallowing down the laughter his words stirred. "My parents died when I was in first grade. In a car crash."

Kevin's eyes went round.

"I moved here to live with my grandmother." She shrugged. "She took good care of me, but it wasn't the same."

"My dad left when I was in second grade."

Annabeth knew the story. Most of Stonewall Crossing did. While Winnie Michaels had a questionable and very public relationship with a married man, Winnie's husband got involved with that man's wife. They left town together—leaving Kevin behind. As far as Annabeth knew, the only good thing about Kevin's father was the reliability of his child support.

"It's hard. And it hurts." She nodded, searching for the right words. She didn't know what to do for Kevin. But she wished he was involved in something, some outlet that would keep him out of his toxic home environment and let off some steam for a few hours each day.

Kevin stared at his hands. "I get angry sometimes."

"We all do." She nodded. "How we deal with the anger is what matters."

"*You* get angry?" From the look on his face, he didn't believe her.

She smiled, nodding. "Yes, I do."

"Doubt it." He shrugged, then asked, "So what's my punishment?"

"What do you think it should be?" she asked.

He looked at her, thinking hard. Finally, he shrugged again.

"I have an idea." She sat forward. "Coach Goebel, are you out there?"

Bryan popped his head in.

"Didn't you say you needed some help after school? Inflating balls, checking gym equipment and scraping the marks off the court?" she asked, hoping he'd take the not-so-subtle hint she was sending him.

"Yes, ma'am." He nodded, walking into her office.

Kevin looked up at him, surprised. "After school?"

"Yep." Coach Goebel nodded.

"For at least the rest of the week," Annabeth added. "I'll have to tell your mom, Kevin."

"Okay." He nodded, looking back and forth between the two adults.

"You can go back to class now," Annabeth said. "But ask your teacher to send Billy to me."

Kevin frowned. "Can't I just apologize to him? He never would have said that if I…if I hadn't made that stuff up about my mom and Mr. Boone."

Annabeth's stomach made another disturbingly loud noise, drawing Bryan's and Kevin's eyes her way. "I think apologizing would be the right thing to do. But I still need to talk to Billy about choosing his words more carefully." She might not be a Winnie Michaels fan, but calling the woman trash wasn't okay. "Please think about what I said though, Kevin. We can't pick who we love—that applies to our friends, too."

Kevin nodded, then hurried out of her office.

She really wanted to rest her head on her desk. And she really wanted to throw up the small amount of cracker she'd just eaten into her trash can. But Coach Goebel was still there, watching her. As ridiculous as it sounded, there was still the chance Bryan Goebel was Ken Branson's ally. And, even though she felt like quitting this very minute, she would not give up this job.

"I didn't mean to interrupt, but I heard him yelling and thought you might need backup." Bryan grinned. "You did a great job with him."

She smiled. "Thank you."

"He can hang out with me and Cody for the rest of the week." He nodded. "Easier to play basketball when there's more players."

Cody. She bit back her groan. She'd just forced her son to give up basketball for the week. Or to spend time with the boy who bullied him the most.

RYDER BALANCED ON the top step of the ladder.

"You know you're not supposed to stand on that, right?" Annabeth said.

"How would you know? Unless you've done the same thing," he replied, draping the strand of lights over the hook he'd hung.

"Ryder." Her exasperated sigh made him chuckle.

He climbed down the ladder, his smile fading. "Annabeth, I got this. Why don't you take Cody home?" She seemed to be getting thinner each day. He knew she was having a hard time keeping her food down, but there had to be something they could do.

"I'm fine." She waved him away, turning to the last box.

"More lights," Irene said. "The last of them."

"Good." Ryder smiled at the parent volunteers, appreciating the work they were doing for their kids. And he didn't mind pitching in—he wanted to be an involved parent. But Annabeth had done enough. She'd already been here twelve hours.

"I can get the last of it." Annabeth opened the box and tilted it onto its side. A huge rat jumped out and skittered across the table where the box rested, leapt to the stage and ran straight for the cover of the curtains. Annabeth jumped back, pinwheeling her arms to steady herself. Ryder was there, his big hands catching her about her waist and steadying her. "Rat! Big big rat."

"Oh, my God," Holly moaned. "I brought that into the school."

Ryder shook his head. "Now we just need to get him out again." His eyes swept over Annabeth. "You okay?"

She nodded. "What do you need?"

"A broom, a trash can, and something large enough to slide under the trash can." He was already looking around the gym.

Annabeth pulled a ring of keys off her hip. "Broom's in the janitor's closet, over there." She pointed in the direction the rat had run.

"Great." He chuckled. "Anyone else wearing boots?" he asked.

"Me," Jim volunteered. "Anyone not wearing boots might as well climb on the tables or get out of the gym. Those bastards bite, and they carry all sorts of bacteria and disease."

Ryder approved of Jim's no-nonsense approach. He took Annabeth's keys and retrieved a broom while Jim found a trash can.

"If we prop open the side door, maybe it'll run out?" Carol said.

The chances of that happening were slim, but he agreed. "Sure." Ryder propped open the side door. As luck would have it, there was a trash can right outside. After a few minutes' search, he located a piece of wood that should work. And that's when the screaming began.

Ryder ran inside to find the rat running around the room, searching for a way out. Maybe they'd get lucky and the damn thing would run outside.

But just as Irene's screaming stopped, Cody, another boy and the coach ran into the room and directly into the path of the rat. Ryder ran faster than he'd ever run, swinging that broom with all the strength he had. He hit the rodent, sending it across the room from Cody. But now the damn thing was mad. Jim approached it, holding the trash can at the ready, but the rat stood on its hind legs and charged the man. Jim backed up, startled, but the rat kept coming.

Ryder kicked into gear. "Coach?" He nodded in the direction of the board.

Thankfully the man was sharp. The coach grabbed the board, approaching Jim and the rat from the right while Ryder took the left.

"You ready?" Ryder asked, hoping Jim realized he was holding the trash can.

Jim snapped out of it then, glaring at the aggressive little rodent before nodding.

"On three?" the coach asked.

It worked. The rat was under the trash can and everyone breathed easier.

"How're we going to get it outside?" the coach asked.

"With this." Ryder took the wood from the coach. "You

hold it? Don't lift it or let it shift, I don't care if we do pinch its toes."

The rat was outside and running across the field in two minutes.

"Should've killed it," the coach muttered under his breath.

"At least it's not in the building." Ryder nodded. "Ryder Boone." He held his hand out.

"Bryan Goebel." The man shook his hand. "Nice to meet you."

"Quick on your feet."

"Wouldn't be much of a coach if I wasn't." The man laughed.

"You okay out here?" Annabeth hurried outside.

"Taken care of," Bryan said.

"Thank you." Annabeth's relief was obvious. "Ryder, I think I will take Cody home now."

Ryder nodded, thankful. She needed to be avoiding stress, resting when she could. He'd spent a lot of time researching pregnancy the past few days and, according to everything he'd read, the first trimester was a fairly risky time. "See you in a bit. I'll cook something when I get there."

She waved, then disappeared inside the building.

"She okay?" Bryan asked.

"She's fine." Ryder glanced at the other man, recognizing the look on Bryan Goebel's face. The longing, the tenderness... Bryan Goebel was sweet on his wife.

Chapter Twelve

Annabeth smoothed the wispy blond hair from Cody's sleeping face. She was still wound up from the evening's events. Yes, she was overreacting, but she was pregnant. Otherwise, seeing that horrible rat running at Cody wouldn't have shaken her up so badly. It was silly. Ryder wouldn't have let anything happen. Deep inside her, she knew that. He hadn't let anything happen. Everyone was safe, because of him.

Ryder...

He'd reacted quickly, without thought. If he'd been rattled or uncertain, she hadn't seen it. He'd had everything in control. Moving with a confidence, and speed, that ratcheted up the already raging attraction she had for her husband.

What really worried her was she knew it was more. She wasn't ready to face what *more* meant. But she was afraid her heart had become intensely involved.

She turned off the hall light and walked into the kitchen, the telltale rumble of thunder outside reminding her of the various leaks in the roof. Lightning flashed in the small window over the kitchen sink. The sink, where Ryder stood. He didn't seem bothered by the coming storm. He was elbows deep in a sink of soapy dishes, humming to whatever country tune was coming from the radio. It looked as though he was content, maybe even a little happy. How she wished that was true.

If she was smart, she'd go to bed. Standing here admiring how his tight gray T-shirt clung to each and every muscle was a bad idea. Her attention lingered on his mighty fine rear. She swallowed, aching with desperate want. If she went over there and wrapped her arms around him, what would happen?

She hesitated for a moment, then did exactly that.

He froze. But not for long. He wiped his hands on a dish towel, then covered hers with his. His hands were hot and damp—encompassing her. She kissed his shoulder, pressing her nose against his back and breathing deep. His head-to-toe shiver surprised her.

Ryder kept her arms in place, even as he turned to face her. He stared down at her, the heat in his gaze challenging the very real warning inside her head. She wanted him and, for whatever reason, right now he wanted her.

His hands cupped her cheeks, tilting her head. The touch of his thumb along her lower lip startled her lips apart. His kiss was fierce. Lips parted, breaths merged, and tongues stoking deep. She melted into him, welcoming the heat that inflamed her. He pressed soft kisses to the corner of her mouth, her cheek, the hollow at the base of her neck. The slight scratch of stubble along her skin plus the sudden tenderness of his kisses had her aching for more. She slipped her hands beneath the hem of his shirt, pressing her palms against his skin.

He pulled his shirt off and let it fall on the floor at their feet.

Her hands traced over his chest, dragging her fingers over each ridge and indentation. Muscles. Golden skin. Raw strength. He was mesmerizing.

"Mrs. Boone," he murmured against her neck. "Option A. We're breaking the rules."

Option A. She blinked. Option A. The plan with no sex

and a temporary marriage. The plan she'd dreamed up to keep things under control. To protect them both. She stared at the wall of muscle that was his stomach and chest, a soft sound of pure frustration escaping her lips.

"Annabeth?" His voice was a low growl.

She wanted him—too much. "I'm sorry," she murmured. "After today... I just... You..." She shook her head. "I crossed a line—" It was hard to meet his gaze.

He was staring down at her, shirtless, gorgeous and barely controlled. "Hell, Princess, cross it." His words were colored with unfiltered hunger.

She sucked in a deep breath, her lungs shuddering at the force of it. The look in his eyes, the heat of his hands and strength of his arms around her. She wanted this. She wanted him. She stepped forward, slipping her hand to the base of his neck and pulling his head down to her.

As their lips met, he lifted her in his arms and carried her to the bedroom. With the heel of his boot, he nudged the door shut. He didn't lay her on the bed, but set her on her feet instead. He knelt in front of her, unbuttoning each of the buttons along her pajama top. When it hung open, he kissed her stomach, along her ribs, under the swell of her breast...leaving a spark of fire in his wake. His hair brushed along her skin, heightening each sensation. And his big hands held her up, solid against her back. His mouth brushed over her nipple, stealing whatever breath she had left.

She shrugged out of her top. It wasn't enough. She needed all of him.

His broken groan shook her where she stood. He wasn't touching her. He didn't have to—his desire was all the encouragement she needed. She started to kneel with him, desperate to feel him against her. But he tugged her pajama bottoms down and stood, the brush of his chest against her own heightening her senses even more.

His hands tangled in her hair as his mouth sealed hers. The touch and slide of his tongue was too much. Her hands fumbled with his belt buckle and jeans. Somehow he managed to get out of them.

They fell back onto the bed, but he rolled them, bringing her on top of him.

She stared down at him, at the beauty of his body, the angles and planes and rugged masculinity. His hands stroked up her arms, his gaze devouring every inch of her. He was just as hungry as she was. His fingers brushed along her neck, wrapping in her long hair to pull her face to his.

His kiss was deep, leaving her lungs empty and her body writhing. He rolled them again, holding her tightly against him. When she dared to look at his face, she was stunned by his expression. Possessiveness—he looked at her as if she was his.

She wanted that…wanted to be his.

He rested on one forearm, his hand cradling her face as he moved slowly into her. She closed her eyes, too overwhelmed by the raw friction, the exquisite pressure. He grew still, his gasping breath cooling her heated skin. She looked at him, at the control he fought for. She kissed his neck, wrapping her legs around his waist. "Make love to me, Ryder."

HE WAS A good lover. He could take his time, drive a woman mad. But something about Annabeth made him lose that, something about her drove *him* mad. She held him tightly, arms and legs and hands. Her body sheathed him so tightly he worried he'd be done before they got started.

He heard her words and looked down at her. Her hands

cradled his face as she arched her back, joining them more deeply in the process. She moaned, her breath hitched, but she never looked away. And he happily drowned in her hazel eyes.

Damn, she was beautiful. Her body and her heart. He loved her. He would love her the way she deserved to be loved.

He moved, soaking up every reaction. Sweet sighs, the roll of her hips, the flush on her skin and the small shudders his touch caused. Watching her was magic, giving him the desire to make it last—to give her what she craved. Her hands tightened on his back, gripping his sides fitfully, dragging a moan from his throat. She was so close. He nuzzled her breast, drawing first one nipple into his mouth, then the next. She whimpered, her nails raking the skin on his back. His mouth on her skin made her crazy. He held her, watching, as every inch of her contracted. Her eyes closed as her neck arched off the pillow. She cried out, threatening Ryder's control. This was about her.

I love you, Annabeth. He pressed kisses along her neck as her cries began to ease. *I love you.*

He let go, finally, moving frantically against her. He held her against him, the feel of her pulling him under. Her hands slid down his chest, gripping his hips in encouragement. The power of his release startled him, rocking him to the core. Her arms held him close until he calmed. But whatever calm his body might be feeling, the throbbing beat of his heart was anything but. He rolled onto his back, careful of her. She turned into his arms, sighing as he pulled her close against him. His heart was still thundering as he pressed a kiss to her temple.

A full-on storm raged outside, a hard rain was falling. But he didn't mind. He was right where he wanted to be, happier than he'd ever been.

"SCHOOLS ARE CLOSED," Annabeth announced, so pleased she wanted to jump up and down like a little girl.

Ryder, sleepy-eyed and barely awake, grinned. He rearranged his pillow, the quilts sliding low to his waist in the process. "You look torn up about it, Princess."

She shook her head. "Not one bit." She slid back into bed beside him, pulling the quilts over them. She frowned then. "You still have to go to the garage?"

He quirked an eyebrow at her. "You suggesting I call in sick?"

She slipped out of the pajama top she'd put on to answer the phone. "I am." She slid on top of him, kissing the tip of his nose.

His hands landed on her rear, sending all sorts of amazing tingles down her back. "Think that can be arranged." His voice was rough and sexy.

She kissed him, loving the way one of Ryder's big hands slid along her back to cradle her head. His lips tugged on her lower lip, and she melted against him hungrily. She moved, gripping his head to tug him close. There was something freeing, knowing they had hours before Cody woke up, hours before they had to face the day.

Ryder groaned softly, pulling her under him.

Her bedroom door creaked as it opened, giving Annabeth just enough time to nudge Ryder off.

"Ma?" Cody's voice was a croak. "M-my bed's wet. W-water coming in."

"Oh, Cody, I'm sorry." She couldn't exactly get up—she was naked.

Ryder slid to the side of the bed. "I'll check it out." Ryder shivered. "Brr. Why don't you climb in the bed there and warm up."

Annabeth tucked the sheets around her before wrapping Cody with quilts. Tom appeared, leaping up to sleep on Cody's chest. It took less than five minutes for Cody to fall asleep, then she slipped into her pajamas.

The house was cold, so she tapped the thermostat and turned the heat up. The unit clicked several times before a gust of warm air came through the floor vents.

Ryder stood on a chair, lightly pressing on the ceiling. A huge patch was clearly soaked through.

"It's bad, isn't it?" She shook her head.

Ryder nodded. "It's bad. Not just in here." He jumped down, took her hand and led her into the small living area. The patch extended for almost half of the room. There were several puddles on the wooden floors, the rhythmic *tap-tap* of water muffled by the water already accumulated.

"How bad?" she asked, refusing to let this ruin the sense of peace she'd woken to.

"New roof bad. New heater, too, probably. And then there's the wiring…" Ryder pushed the hair from her shoulder, enfolding her in his arms. "We should move out to the ranch for a while."

Annabeth stared up at him. "We…we can't inconvenience your dad that way."

"It's no inconvenience, Princess." He kissed her forehead, then her nose. "We can't stay here, it's not safe. This is gonna be a major cleanup, too." He looked at the roof. "Be a good idea to put most of this in storage, for now."

"All I wanted was a morning in bed with you." She frowned. "Talk about a mood-killer."

"There are beds there. Big, comfy beds." The muscle in his jaw was working. "Morning, afternoon, night, I'm there." He kissed her, leaving no doubt that he meant it.

She burrowed into his arms, ignoring the leak and the puddles and the cold for a minute longer.

"I'll call my dad." Ryder's voice was muffled in her hair.

"It's barely six," she argued.

"He's up, I guarantee it." He smiled, his hold easing.

"I guess I'll get dressed and see about finding packing materials." Her brain was already making lists of things she'd need to do. "What a mess."

"Nothing that can't be fixed." He tilted her head back. "How's your stomach?"

She smiled. "Hungry."

"Good." He headed for the kitchen and pulled out a skillet and eggs. "Breakfast will be ready in a bit."

She watched him, smiling at his outfit. Boxer shorts, boots and his thick work coat. And he still managed to look hot. "You want your pants?" She laughed.

He smiled at her. "Am I distracting you?"

She cocked her head. Did he know that she wanted to drag him back to bed? She sighed. The bed where Cody was now soundly sleeping. "Yes, you are," she admitted.

His jaw was working again, and she liked it. "The couch isn't wet," he suggested, an egg in his hand.

She rolled her eyes, but her breath was unsteady. "What am I going to do with you, Ryder Boone?"

He grinned, his signature I'm-going-to-rock-your-world grin. "I have some suggestions—"

She held up her hand, heading from the kitchen. "Stop." But she was giggling.

Chapter Thirteen

Ryder stood watching his wife mingle with the people of Stonewall Crossing. He knew she was exhausted. Neither one of them had been getting a lot of sleep recently. Between the storm, the damage to the house and moving into the Lodge, he and Annabeth hadn't had much time alone. But he felt confident he was making headway with his plan—destroy Option A.

Sure, living under the same roof as his father took some getting used to. But Annabeth was one of those people who kept the peace, without even trying. And Cody was settling in. His father had given them the only suite in the Lodge, so he had his own room—even if he'd spent last night sleeping between them. Overall, life was damn good.

"I think she gets prettier every time I see her." John Hardy clapped him on the back.

Ryder nodded. "No one prettier."

John chuckled.

Ryder shook his head. "I'm whipped."

"That's all right." John laughed. "A man would be downright foolish not to be with a woman like that."

Ryder watched Annabeth laugh. He couldn't agree more.

"I need to talk to you, if you have a minute?" John asked.

"Yes, sir," he agreed, leading John into one of the smaller rooms off the great room.

"My kids have all up and moved, you know that. None of them are interested in my line of work, anyway. You are." John paused. "Now, with Annabeth and your family, I figure you might be willing to take on the garage."

Ryder stared at him. John Hardy had always believed in him, giving him a job and a roof over his head since he was eighteen. He was a good man, someone Ryder was proud to know. It hadn't been easy to say no to JJ, and JJ wasn't ready to give up yet, but Ryder knew he was where he belonged. And now this.

John held up his hand. "I know you're sore about staying put, not getting to work with JJ, but hear me out. If the garage was yours, you could do the bodywork and custom jobs you've always wanted to. Stonewall Crossing might be a little off the main road, but they'd come—for your work."

His own garage. With an established clientele. Here, not starting over. He was getting everything he always wanted.

"Just think about it. Seems like you're settling down all right, putting down those roots you've never wanted to plant before. This might help with that." John nodded, clapping Ryder on the shoulder again. "I'll let you stew awhile while I hunt down some more of that honey lemonade Fisher made."

Ryder nodded, wishing he was better with words. "You're a generous man, John."

John smiled. "And you're a good man who loves an engine almost as much as I do." He nodded once then headed off in search of Fisher's lemonade.

"Hiding?" Hunter asked, coming in as John left. "Renata really did invite everyone, didn't she?"

"The entire damn town."

Hunter grinned. "Your wife's looking for you."

His wife. The woman he took every opportunity to touch, to kiss and hold.

He smiled, heading back to the great room. There was no shortage of activity. The ice storm had delayed the party a week. And now, with the cold and ice hanging on, the party couldn't spill out onto the series of decks that ran down the hill behind the Lodge, the way Renata had originally planned. Add in the endlessly revolving servers coming to and from the kitchen, and it was a little too close for comfort. His brother Fisher sat with Cody and Eli and a few other kids, making paper airplanes out of Renata's fancy wedding announcements. His father and a few of his cronies were seated along the back wall, their chairs grouped around the massive fireplace. His other brother, Archer, had been cornered by two women with single daughters. To marry a Boone in Stonewall Crossing was pretty damn close to becoming Hill Country royalty.

"Hey." Annabeth smiled as soon as she saw him. It warmed him through, seeing her look at him like that.

"How're you holding up?" He took her hand in his and stared at her. She was, without a doubt, the most beautiful woman he'd ever seen. And when she smiled up at him like that, she made him feel like the only man in the world. A man who wanted to kiss her more than anything. His fingers laced through hers.

"Ryder," she chastised him. "You shouldn't look at me like that."

Ryder laughed. "Like what?"

She turned to face him, flushed. "Like *that*..." Her voice was unsteady.

He grinned. "I don't know what you think I'm thinking. I was thinking about me." He kissed the back of her hand. "And you—"

"Exactly." She nodded, wiggling her fingers.

"And Cody going fishing when it warms up," he added,

watching her cheeks turn a deep scarlet. "What did you think I was thinking?" he teased.

"Nothing." She shook her head. "Nice to know I'm in your thoughts."

He slid an arm around her waist. When was she not in his thoughts? Every decision he'd made had been with her in mind. He stroked her side, getting accustomed to the way his heart reacted to her. "You are, Princess," he whispered.

She smiled up at him.

"Ma." Cody tugged on Annabeth's denim skirt. "Can I take Eli to my room? To play with Tom? Or watch a m-movie?"

"'Course you can," Ryder replied.

Cody looked at Ryder, then Annabeth. She nodded, ruffling his hair. "'Kay, thanks." The two ran out of the room.

"Can I go with them?" Ryder asked.

"Nope." She shook her head. "You're not leaving me." Her smile faded into a frown.

He didn't have time to ask what was wrong—his father was headed their way. Once he saw the people his father had in tow, he realized what Teddy Boone was up to. He and his father might not see eye to eye on some things, but they both wanted to help Annabeth any way they could.

"Annabeth, you remember Mack?"

Mack enveloped Annabeth in a hug. "Good to see marriage is agreeing with you, Mrs. Boone."

"Well, thank you for marrying us," she said, smiling.

His father grinned. "Don't know if you know Don and Haddie Miles?"

"In passing, I think." Annabeth was all warm smiles and handshakes. "It's a pleasure."

Pleasure might be pushing it, but Ryder just smiled. Haddie Miles was one of the few women who used to rub his mother the wrong way. Hell, she was an older version of Winnie Michaels.

"Look at you, Ryder," Haddie said. "What a fine man you've turned into. Either Annabeth doesn't know what a rascal you are, or she's decided to try to redeem you."

Ryder didn't flinch. "She knows all about my past, ma'am. And she's shown me the error of my ways." Haddie smirked, but the men present turned a universally appreciative gaze upon his wife.

"And this old pain in the rear is Charles Sharp." Teddy stepped back so the gnarled older gentleman could shake Annabeth's hand.

"Call me Cutter," the old man said as he waved Teddy back. "My eyesight's not so good," he grumbled, coming to stand inches from Annabeth. His milky eyes widened. "Hell's bells, boy, you married well." Cutter shook his head. "And she's the principal, too, Teddy? The one there's all the fuss over?"

"Cutter—" Haddie shushed the older man.

Ryder felt Annabeth stiffen and took her hand in his.

"I see why now." Cutter laughed. "Ol' prune face Branson can't stand to be put in his place by any woman. One that looks like this? Hooey, gotta chap his hide."

It took everything Ryder had to swallow his laugh.

"I don't think you're supposed to talk about school board business here, Cutter," Mack said, trying to rein the older man in.

Cutter made a rude sound. "Like to see 'em try to fire me." His eyes narrowed as he assessed Annabeth again. "Why do you think you're the best one for the job, Annabeth Boone?"

"Now, Cutter…" Don placed a hand on the other man's arm.

"I'll leave her be." Cutter shrugged out from under the other man's touch. "After she answers the question."

Ryder saw the look of panic on Annabeth's face. He knew, deep down, she was tempted to use this opportunity to sell herself. She wanted the job and she'd worked hard to get it. And, as she reminded him time and again, the job helped her make ends meet. Not that she needed to worry about that now.

"Mr. Sharp, I can't, in good faith, answer that question. Not here. I know I'm not the only candidate." She glanced at each of them while leaning in to him. His arm slipped around her waist, offering her the support she was looking for. "I'd feel wrong, unethical, trying to get ahead like that."

Cutter made another rude sound. "You can bet your sweet ass Branson wouldn't have said that." He laughed.

"I expect you'll be taking your honeymoon this summer?" Mack asked.

Ryder smiled. A honeymoon? Sounded like a good idea. Everyone would expect it. And it would give him the time he needed with Annabeth. "The sooner the better," he agreed.

"Where are you thinking about going? My daughter, June, and her husband went to Paris. They said it was awful. The people were rude and everything cost too much. One time—" Haddie was off. She was a talker, he remembered that much.

Annabeth shifted from one foot to the other, her hand pressing his tightly. She did it again, harder. He glanced at her, noting how pale she looked. He steadied her with his arm, taking her hand in his. Her fingers were icy cold. He scanned the room, looking for help. He caught the eye of Josie, chatting happily with Lola and Flo. He tilted his head slightly, hoping Josie would get the message. He saw her frown, glance at Annabeth and head their way.

"Annabeth?" Josie interrupted. "I'm so sorry. I need to steal you."

"Oh? Of course." Annabeth smiled warmly at the group. "We'll make sure not to go to Paris, Mrs. Miles. Thank you for sharing that with me. It was lovely to see you all."

He wanted to go with her, but he knew better. Josie would take care of her.

"What are your plans, Ryder?" Mr. Miles asked. "Now you've got a wife and son, I imagine you're looking into bigger and better career opportunities."

"Ryder's a damn fine mechanic," his father interrupted. "John Hardy's always singing his praises. And he should. Works hard, for John and when he's helping out here." His father nodded at him. Ryder tried not to stare back, stunned by his father's words. "When he's not riding bulls that is," his father added reluctantly.

"I've seen him ride," Mack joined in. "Had me on my feet counting down. Damn impressive."

"Lucky bastard," Cutter growled. "Love your job, love your wife—that's a damn good life."

"Amen." Teddy nodded.

"Ain't that the truth," Mack added.

Ryder couldn't have said it better himself.

"Did you eat this morning?" Josie asked her. "You look so pale."

"I ate, I just didn't keep much of it down. But I did eat." Annabeth smiled. "I'm fine. Just got a little overheated I think."

"It's awfully stuffy," Josie agreed. "Still, you should probably try to eat something." She pressed against the kitchen counter as one of the servers rushed past, carrying a large tray. "None of this looks good?"

Annabeth eyed the chilled shrimp, the canapés and

mini éclairs, and tiny cornbread thimbles full of chili. She shook her head. "The smells are enough."

"How about some chicken noodle soup?" Josie had the refrigerator open.

Annabeth thought about it. "Sure."

"You go wait in Teddy's office so you have a moment's peace," Josie told her. "Go the back way, down this hall. I'll warm some up and bring it to you."

"Thank you, Josie." She hugged her friend.

"Your husband was worried about you." Josie held her by the shoulders. "I know things aren't settled between you," she whispered, "but I know he loves you."

Annabeth swallowed the lump in her throat.

"Go on." Josie shooed her in the direction of the hall.

Annabeth went, flopping into the overstuffed leather chair with a sigh. She peered out the window, appreciating the view. From here, Teddy could see land. No houses or roads or fences, just his property. Property that had been in the Boone family for generations. It must be a humbling thing, to be the caretaker of such a vast property. But he had his sons to help. All of them. She hoped, in time, Ryder would find a way to make peace with his family. There'd always been tension whenever the Boones were together. Now, not so much…but they were a long way from the united family they could be. The sort of family she wanted.

She stood, pacing the floor. She was an idiot. She wanted a home and family. She wanted a husband, someone she could build a life with. She wanted to believe Ryder could be that man, but she couldn't shake the feeling that she was headed toward another heartbreak.

Ryder was Ryder. There were times she wondered if he'd changed—if she and Cody were what he wanted. That's what she wanted to believe. But when the twins were teething, Cody was sick and she had to work a twelve-hour day, would he still be here? Was he ready for that?

Now was not the time to give up being practical.

He'd always been motivated by his loyalty to Greg, not his feelings for her. She needed to remember that. Her heart needed to accept that.

Her stomach clenched and she pressed both her hands against it, stifling a groan. She was not a fan of morning sickness or throwing up. She couldn't wait for this first trimester to be over. Almost there—

"Annabeth?" Hunter stood just inside the door. "Are you okay?"

She straightened, smoothing the white linen tunic over her stomach nervously. "Fine. Just a little overheated."

Hunter stood there. "You need anything?"

"No." She shook her head.

"Do you want me to get Ryder?" he asked, the intensity of his expression unnerving her.

"I'm fine."

He smiled. "Dad's friends can be a lot to handle."

She laughed. "That's an understatement. I hope I didn't disappoint your father."

"I wouldn't worry about that, Annabeth. We're all happy you're part of the family."

Josie arrived, carrying soup and crackers. "Here. Maybe this will agree with your stomach."

"I thought you were overheated?" Hunter asked, cocking an eyebrow.

Josie shot Hunter a look, placed the soup on the table by the window and handed Annabeth the linen napkin she carried.

Annabeth watched the silent exchange between the husband and wife.

"I didn't ask because I didn't want you to have to lie," Hunter said.

"I wouldn't have lied, if you'd asked." Josie crossed the room, sliding her arms around Hunter's neck.

He sighed, rubbing his nose against Josie's.

"I'm guessing I'm going to be an uncle?" Hunter asked, never looking away from his wife.

Annabeth stared into her soup, too nauseated to eat. "Yes."

Hunter looked at her. "I can't say I'm surprised."

"He wants to do the right thing," she said, wanting to defend Ryder.

Hunter smiled. "Annabeth, Ryder's my little brother. I've watched him grow up, I know him—whether he likes it or not."

She crossed her arms, frowning. "He's a good man—"

"With you, yes," Hunter agreed. "You bring out the best in him, always have."

She blinked back the tears that stung her eyes. Even if Ryder loved her, did it matter? Loving her wouldn't change who he was. She wanted to believe it.

"You're worried?" Hunter asked.

"Can you blame her?" Josie asked. "Even when people are congratulating her, it's like they're also warning her about him."

Annabeth smiled, nodding.

"What do you think?" Hunter asked her.

She chewed on her lip, willing the tears away. "He's been trying to take care of me and Cody, for Greg. Now, this… He's trapped." Her hands brushed over her stomach. "I know him, too, Hunter. He's a restless spirit. One I won't keep for long."

Ryder came through the door, his face lined with worry.

"You okay?" He crossed to her, wrapping his arms around her. "Feeling all right?"

"I'm fine," she murmured, turning her face into his shirt.

"I thought she might want some peace and quiet," Josie spoke.

Ryder turned, but his hold on her didn't ease. "Thanks, Josie. Hunter." She felt Ryder's hands tighten on her arms. "Guess you know?"

"That Josie and I are going to have a niece or nephew?" Hunter's voice was calm. "Yep. Congratulations. I'm happy for you both."

Ryder's grip eased on her. She knew Hunter's opinion was important to Ryder, no matter how much he tried to pretend otherwise.

Her stomach gurgled loudly. "Sorry. My stomach isn't cooperating," she moaned.

He looked down at her. "Did you try eating?"

She pointed at the soup. "Josie just made that for me."

He let her go, nodding at the bowl.

"You're so bossy," she teased, sitting. She lifted the bowl, grimacing at the smell of celery and chicken broth.

"At least try." Josie sat on the footstool.

"I can't eat with all of you watching me." Annabeth laughed.

"Come on, Ryder, let's head back. It won't look good if you're both missing," Hunter said. "You need anything else?"

Annabeth shook her head, trying not to laugh at her frowning husband. "I'm fine."

"Renata has some slide show she put together," Hunter added. "About the two of you. When you're ready."

"She does?" Annabeth stirred the bowl, swallowing a spoonful. It was surprisingly good. She managed to have some more, the mild flavors soothing her sour stomach. She waved them off, enjoying half of her bowl before deciding she was done. Josie tried to feed her some crackers, but she didn't want to push it. She felt much better when she headed back to the party.

Annabeth helped move chairs around in the great room, but there wasn't enough room for everyone to sit.

"Come on, Flo, right up front." Ryder parked Flo's wheelchair front and center.

"Best seat in the house," Flo exclaimed. "You're spoiling me."

"Part of my job," Ryder teased.

Annabeth watched, touched by his thoughtfulness.

"Annabeth, you give this boy extra kisses for taking care of me." Flo shook her finger at her.

Annabeth laughed as Ryder pulled her into his lap, in a chair beside Flo.

"Extra kisses sound good," he whispered in her ear. With one look, he made her feel beautiful…and teary eyed.

Renata lowered the large screen the Lodge used for business retreats or movie nights. As the lights dimmed, Cody and Eli scampered in to sit on the floor and lean back against Ryder's chair.

Music started and the title sprang up: "Annabeth and Ryder's Love Story."

Everyone oohed over their baby pictures. Ryder was adorable, there was no denying it. She'd never seen images of a young Teddy and Mags Boone. He was handsome and she was amazingly beautiful. A quick glance at Teddy gave her pause. It was clear the old man still loved and missed his wife.

The montage of their growing-up years was bittersweet. While Annabeth's parents were absent, pictures of Greg were everywhere.

"Is that Dad?" Cody asked after one hilarious picture of the three of them covered in mud, holding a puppy high.

Annabeth nodded. "That was his dog."

"What h-happened?" Cody asked.

"The dog slid down the riverbank, and the water started to rise. The dog couldn't get back up—"

"Your mom climbed down before we could stop her," Ryder interrupted.

"But it got them down there with me," Annabeth added. "And the dog was safe."

"Safe. But all four of 'em were covered in mud," Flo interjected.

Cody laughed, shaking his head.

Annabeth ruffled his hair, smiling at the top of his head. She needed to tell more stories about Greg, so he'd know his father.

"Oh, look at that." The amusement in Lola's voice drew Annabeth's attention back to the screen. She was at one of the town festivals, manning a kissing booth. She was kissing Ryder. She didn't remember that. She glanced at Ryder, who was grinning.

By the time the pictures entered the high school years, it was clear that Annabeth was wild about Greg. But Ryder was there, too. At graduation, he was smiling at her. At one of the vacations to the beach, she'd fallen asleep on his shoulder while Greg was fishing. When Cody was born, Ryder was in the hospital. He was cradling Cody, looking at him with such awe and adoration it was hard to believe Cody wasn't his. It was a good thing Ryder had been living in Las Vegas when she'd gotten pregnant, or people would undoubtedly talk.

There were more. Cody working on his toy car while Ryder worked on the real ones. Ryder taking Cody fishing with his brothers. And Ryder staring at her when she was talking to Grandma Flo. It was from a few years back, and Grandma Flo wasn't in her wheelchair yet.

The look on his face took her breath away.

"I was quite a looker." Flo's announcement made everyone laugh.

So many occasions and events, whether he was standing alongside her or somewhere in the background—Ryder was there.

A blank slide popped up, the words "Congratulations, Annabeth and Ryder! Wishing you a life of love and laughter!" scrolling slowly by.

Her heart was racing by the time the last picture popped up. It was a picture of them dancing.

"I took that one," John Hardy called out.

Cody hopped up, hugging Ryder, then hugging her. "Love you."

She hugged him tightly. "I love you, too."

"Picture!" Lola was up, holding her phone out. "Since there aren't any wedding pictures, we should take some here."

"Great idea," Renata agreed.

Before she knew what was happening, the chairs were cleared away and she and Ryder were standing in front of the fireplace.

They took so many pictures her cheeks hurt from smiling. But she understood how important it was, to have something tangible from this day. When she'd lost Greg and his memory seemed to be slipping away, she'd pulled out the old albums for comfort. She had no right to deprive Teddy or the Boones. As she and Ryder and Cody gathered around Flo's chair, she was happy, too.

"So happy for you precious dears." Flo kissed them each on the cheek. "Now get to work on more grandbabies. Right, Teddy?"

Teddy blushed furiously. "Well, now, Flo, when they're ready..." he trailed off.

"We'll get on it." Ryder smiled.

"I want a brother." Cody nodded, all wide-eyed excitement.

Annabeth laughed; she couldn't help it.

Ryder winked at Cody. "We'll see what we can do."

"One more, just the happy couple." Renata waved everyone else aside, waiting for Fisher to wheel Grandma Flo back to Lola.

"You may kiss the bride," Mack called out from the back of the room.

Ryder faced her, smoothing her hair from her face to give her a quick kiss.

"Ryder Boone, you can do better than that," Flo chastised, making everyone laugh.

Annabeth giggled, nervous. Partly because of the people watching and partly because of the way he was looking at her. He kissed her softly, sweetly, his hands coming up to cup her face. She covered his hands with hers and the kiss lingered. It was all too easy to get lost in the heat between them. She wanted to give in, to get lost in him... until the whistles and catcalls started up.

Ryder broke away, pressing a kiss to her forehead and sliding his arm around her shoulders. Annabeth could tell he wasn't thrilled over all the attention, but he was trying. It didn't help that half the people congratulating them insisted on bringing up Ryder's history with women. Even Flo got in on the act. She couldn't stop her growing irritation. But Ryder kept smiling, shaking hands long after she was done.

"You feeling okay?" he asked.

"I'm feeling fine." She hadn't meant to snap.

"What's wrong?"

She looked into his pale blue eyes. "I'm frustrated."

"I'm getting that." He nodded. "About?"

She stared at her feet. "I'm tired of hearing about...your past." She shook her head. "Everyone has a past, but some are more *colorful* than others." She smiled at him. "But I don't see anyone else getting so much grief. Doesn't it bother you?"

"Sure." His gaze traveled over her face. "Only thing I can do is prove I've changed."

Had he changed? She hoped so. She couldn't think of anything she wanted more. Her heart hurt.

"Actions speak louder than words, Mrs. Boone." He caressed the side of her face. "Seems like the only thing I can do is love you until no one in Stonewall Crossing can doubt it." He smiled at her, shaking his head. "No one. Not even you, Princess."

Chapter Fourteen

Ryder stood under the shower, letting the steaming water pour over him. He was tired. The past week he'd had a complete transmission overhaul on a two-day turnaround. And in the evenings, he and Hunter had been riding the fence line to replace any posts the storms had damaged. Times like this reminded him just how big the ranch was.

DB had called him about a rodeo, but he'd turned him down without a second thought.

Annabeth came into the bathroom. "There's a phone call for you." She tapped on the shower door. "The whales said the water level is getting a little low and asked that you wrap up your marathon shower."

Ryder laughed, turning off the water. "Damn whales."

He heard Annabeth giggle.

He pushed open the glass door and wrapped a towel around his waist. Annabeth was brushing her teeth, in an oversize tank top. He stood, enjoying the view. He needed to spend more time feeding her. She was beautiful, no doubt about it, but she could use more meat on her bones.

"Want a kiss?" she asked, turning toward him with a toothpaste-sudsy mouth.

He didn't hesitate, closing the gap between them in three steps and pulling her against him.

"Ryder, no!" she squealed, laughing. "Joke."

He bent his head, dropping a kiss on her nose, then let her go. He stared down at her baby bump. His baby bump. She was starting to show. And he loved it. His hands covered her stomach, smoothing along the sides of her rounded belly to support the underside. Something about the sight lodged a knot in his throat.

"Give me a sec?" Annabeth asked, slipping from his hold long enough to rinse the toothpaste from her mouth. She took his hands and placed them back on her stomach.

"Doctor appointment is next week?" he asked, stroking her stomach. According to the baby book, she had a lot going on inside of her right now.

She nodded. "Tuesday at four thirty."

"I'll be there." He smiled. "I'm going to kiss you now." He pressed a soft kiss to her mouth, her breath hitching. He wanted to believe she wanted him, that their incredible night together was the first of many incredible nights together. But he still had to work at getting kisses. Or holding hands. Or sleeping with her head on his shoulder every night. He kissed the tip of her nose. "If we're going to get to the meeting on time, that's all you're getting, Princess."

She sighed.

"Nervous?" he asked. She might be cool as a cucumber, but he was tied in knots about the school board meeting. She wanted this job. And that meant he wanted her to have it.

She shrugged, pulling a compact from the lemon-print bag with all her toiletries. "No point being nervous." She met his gaze in the mirror. "They've already made their decision." But she was staring at his chest, distracted and dazed and...aroused?

He stepped behind and slid his arms around her, holding her. "Guess so." He dropped a kiss on her shoulder. She smelled good, but she tasted better. He threw caution to the wind and slid her bra strap aside, kissing the skin beneath. He groaned and stepped back, amazed at how quickly his body responded to her. He risked looking at her in the mirror and groaned again.

Her eyes were round, her breathing harsh and unsteady. The flush of desire on her cheeks made him ache.

"What was that?" Her voice was rough and sexy as hell.

"Princess." He ran his fingers down her back, loving the way she shivered. So she wanted him. But did she love him? Could she love him? He cleared his throat. "Sometimes I forget about Option A. Or I think we should burn it or let Cody feed it into the shredder in your office and never talk about it again…"

Her brow creased, her hazel gaze boring into his. She nodded. "I need clothes." She laughed, an unsteady breathy sound, and hurried out of the bathroom. "Think a lot of people will turn out?"

He followed her into their bedroom and pulled out a pair of pressed slacks and a button-down oxford. "With the announcement and all, I imagine parents will be curious to see what's decided."

In true Texas-weather fashion, the temperature had climbed from the thirties to the eighties in a matter of days. She looked like spring in the yellow polka-dot sundress and white sweater she pulled on.

"Things are starting to get tight." She turned, pushing the sleeves of her sweater up. "Is it… Am I obvious?"

Too him, she was perfection. Still a little too thin, maybe. But he suspected her stomach was only obvious to him because he knew she was carrying his babies. "Nope. You look beautiful."

She rolled her eyes, sat on the edge of the bed and buckled her heels. "Are you sure your dad doesn't mind watching Cody tonight—"

"Annabeth," Ryder interrupted, tucking his shirt into

his slacks. "Dad's tickled pink he's got a boy around that's interested in model cars again." He tugged on his boots. "They probably won't even know we're gone."

Annabeth stood, smoothing down her skirt. "I don't like imposing—"

"You're not imposing." He gripped her shoulders. "You're family."

She nodded, though the smile on her face wasn't convincing.

"Ready?" he asked, surprised at how edgy he felt. "You're meeting with the board privately, before the community meeting?"

She nodded, but her smile cooled, as if she was bracing for something.

"Hey." He took her hand. "Everything's going to be okay." He squeezed her hand. "Right?"

There was something in her huge hazel eyes he didn't understand—and it scared him. He didn't like fear, wasn't accustomed to it. If something scared him, he faced it head-on and fought it. What was there to fight? How could he win her?

Tonight he'd know if she needed him or not. If she got the job, she could take care of things on her own and she'd expect him to go. If she didn't get the job…well, she'd be devastated. Either way, he couldn't win. And there wasn't a damn thing he could do about it.

"Right." She headed out of the bedroom, tense and rigid.

He followed, his stomach full of lead and his heart heavy. No matter what happened tonight, he wouldn't give up. No matter what happened tonight, Annabeth was his wife. He'd figure out a way to fight—to hold on to her and their family. He had to.

ANNABETH SNUCK INTO the dim high school auditorium and scanned the crowd. The meeting had already started and there seemed to be some discussion about team sports. She saw Ryder instantly—and felt the air leaving her lungs.

She got the job. She would stay the principal. After their brief meeting, she'd gone to the bathroom to pull herself together.

Option A said he'd move to Dallas and take his dream job. Option A. The one she didn't want.

She made her way to where he sat, his words replaying in her mind. *Everything's going to be okay...* How was anything going to be okay? She was beyond excited about the job, but there was so much more at stake.

"Hey," he whispered when he saw her.

She smiled at him, biting her bottom lip to stop the quiver. She saw the slight furrow of his brow and willed herself to really smile. It would have been easier if he wasn't looking at her, waiting to hear. She stared right back, memorizing the chiseled brow and strong jaw. She was in love with him—but she'd have to let him go.

He winked.

Her heart stuttered a little, but she rolled her eyes as if it was no big deal.

"You good?" he whispered.

She wrinkled her nose, smoothing her hands over her stomach. But, for the first time in weeks, her nausea had nothing to do with the babies inside.

His expression went from playful to intense. "Need to go?"

She shook her head.

He nodded, but didn't look convinced. "So?" he prodded.

"As you all know, we've been interviewing candidates for the principal position at Stonewall Crossing Elementary School. This has been quite a process." Haddie Miles's voice rang out. "And we truly appreciate the quality of excellence each of our candidates had to offer our fair town."

Cutter grumbled something, clearly impatient with Haddie's speech.

"That being said, we felt that one candidate's experience, familiarity with our community and references were the perfect fit for our fine school." Haddie turned to the gentlemen of the school board, who all seemed content to let Haddie do the talking. "We would like to thank Mr. Ken Branson of Stonewall Crossing, Mrs. Olivia Sanchez of Glendale, Illinois, Mr. William Marshall of San Antonio and Mrs. Annabeth Boone of Stonewall Crossing for your time and patience throughout our deliberation."

Ryder's hand captured hers. His fingers threaded with hers, warm and soothing… She glanced at their entwined fingers. If not getting the job meant she kept Ryder, she didn't want it. If she could keep him… But that wasn't true, either. She wanted him to stay because he wanted to, not because he had to.

She looked at Ryder again.

It was too late, the damage was done. She'd been so naive. Marrying her had been the easy part. Divorcing her would cost him…everything. No one would ever forgive him, no matter what she said. And it would be her fault. She swallowed down the bile that nearly choked her.

She never wanted to hurt him.

So many hearts would be hurt. Their families'. Cody. Hers…

Why had she ever agreed to this?

"We are pleased to offer the position of principal to Mrs. Annabeth Boone." Haddie Miles paused. "Where are you, Mrs. Boone?" She shielded her eyes and peered into the auditorium.

Annabeth stood, waving.

A smattering of applause broke out in the auditorium, making her look around for the first time. Quite a turnout, especially for Stonewall Crossing. The loyal volunteers were there. Most of the elementary staff sat on the far side of the dimly lit auditorium. No wonder she hadn't noticed them when she came in. Ken Branson wasn't pleased, but he was wearing his plastic smile.

"Mrs. Boone, the board has your contract for you to review. And, of course, you'll have two weeks to decide if you still want to be principal." Haddie laughed and Annabeth sat down.

The audience laughed, as well.

Annabeth wanted to cry, but forced herself to smile.

"As that concludes the board's official business, we'll open the floor to questions and concerns. Please remember to follow the rules…" Haddie carried on.

She stared straight ahead, smiling at the wall in front of her. She had to keep smiling, even though she wanted to cry.

"Told you so," Ryder whispered, kissing her cheek softly. "Congratulations."

"You did." She glanced at him, more nervous now than she'd been all night. It was real, she had the job. She'd be okay. She could take care of Grandma Flo and Cody. And the twins. He could go now. The sting in her eyes caught her off guard.

"Meeting adjourned." Haddie Miles whacked a gavel on the table with a surprising amount of force.

"Congratulations," Janet said as she slipped into the row behind them.

"Yay!" Janet was there, and Lori and Abigail.

"So glad it's you," Lori added. "You'll take care of us."

Grandma Flo's words went through her head. *Sometimes hiding your feelings is better than showing them.*

This was definitely one of those times. "Thank you," she tried to gush. "I'm so relieved." She let go of Ryder's hand, turning in her seat to smile at them all.

"Congrats." Bryan Goebel sat behind Ryder. "Haven't been here long, but it's plain to see you're the right choice." He laughed. "Just don't tell Ken I said that."

"Thanks, Bryan." She paused. "Has Ken mentioned the opening? Coach Hernandez decided it was time to retire after all."

Bryan nodded. "Good to know."

She spent the next few minutes accepting congratulations, all the while wishing she was home in bed. And not at the Lodge, but in her own tiny house. She wanted to cry it out, pull herself together and attack tomorrow with purpose. The sooner she and Cody were back in their tiny house, back in their routine, the sooner things would start to feel normal again. Normal—without Ryder.

For now, she kept up the small talk, aware of Ryder's strong hand on the small of her back. What would she do without his strength?

"Mrs. Boone?" Haddie called her.

"I'll be back." She glanced at Ryder.

"I'll wait." He was watching her, a mix of concern and pride on his face. "Ice cream?"

She nodded, smiling.

He smiled back, a heart-thumping, knee-weakening smile.

"I'll hurry." She made her way to the stage, hoping she carried herself with some sense of confidence.

"Annabeth—" Ken caught her before she reached the steps. "Congratulations. Can't say I'm not a little disappointed, but there's no one I'd rather lose to."

She smiled, taking the hand he offered her. "Thank you, Ken, that means a lot."

He nodded, shaking her hand before joining his wife.

"Here's the paperwork." Cutter pushed a manila envelope across the table. "Too much money if you ask me, but no one did."

"Congratulations again, Mrs. Boone." Haddie shook her hand. "Meant to give this to you earlier but *Cutter* forgot it in his truck."

"Thank you, Mrs. Miles," she replied, shaking the woman's hand.

"First a wedding, now the job." Mack shook her hand. "I'd have to say you're having a good year."

And babies. She nodded.

The conversation was short. Review the offer and let them know in two weeks. The board did have some thoughts on some building additions they'd like to discuss with her, but that could wait until all the paperwork was signed. And they wanted to determine next year's calendar, discuss a new track surface and options for teacher training. None of which seemed to matter right now. By the time she climbed into Ryder's truck, she was on the verge of tears. She closed her eyes and rested her head on the back of the seat.

Ryder climbed in and turned on the heat, but didn't move. "You going to take the job?"

She opened her eyes, staring up at the lining of the truck cab. "Of course."

"You don't seem happy." His tone was neutral.

"I am. Besides, life isn't always about doing what you want to," she argued. "It's about doing what you need to do."

"Okay." He paused, driving two blocks before asking, "Why do you need this job?"

She looked at him, swallowing hard.

"I was watching you tonight, Princess. You were happy

until the meeting. Tired, yes. Stressed, sure. But once they said your name, you looked like Tom when Cody goes to school. Like you're losing something?"

"I don't know what you're talking about." She frowned at him. *I am losing you.* "I've been managing. I can do this."

He moved across the bench seat and took her hands in his. "Damn right, you can." His brow furrowed. "But you don't have to if you don't want to."

She looked at their hands. "Ryder."

"Talk to me," he said, his voice low.

She shook her head.

"You don't have to pretend with me." His words twisted her heart.

She glanced at him, but it was too hard. "I have the weight of the world on my shoulders. Medical bills that are sky-high—"

"I didn't know—"

"A house that would probably be better off flattened than repaired—"

"Annabeth," he tried again.

"A son, a sweet precious boy, who needs building up—and someone to look up to. This job pays significantly more than my teacher's salary. I don't know what the offer is exactly—" she tapped the manila envelope in her lap "—but it will take care of the things I *must* take care of." She shook her head. "Yes, this job is long hours and crazy parents and rats in the cafeteria…but it also provides the one thing my children need. Stability. With the twins coming…" She drew in a shuddering breath. "I need stability. We need it." She pressed her hand to her stomach. "If something falls apart, I can take care of it. *I* have to take care of *my* family."

The quiet grew, filling the truck cab until Annabeth couldn't take it.

Ryder slid back into his seat and turned on the truck. He pulled through the soda shop on the way home, buying her a double dip of her favorite—butter pecan. But he didn't say a word all the way home.

The top scoop of ice cream had all but melted by the time she went inside. Cody was so excited she gave the remainder to him, making him promise not to get too sticky since it was still a while until bath time. Ryder took Cody into the kitchen to prevent splattering the wooden floors with ice cream drips.

"How did it go?" Teddy asked.

Something about Teddy Boone's question broke the dam. Maybe it was the glimmer of pride she saw on his face. Or the fact that she'd never had a father to look at her that way. Or that she was overwhelmed and exhausted.

Whatever it was, she burst into tears, her legs giving out beneath her. She flopped onto one of the leather sofas and pressed her hands over her mouth so Cody wouldn't hear her, but she couldn't stop the sobs.

Teddy sat beside her, hugging her against his barrel chest. "It's all right, Annabeth. It's all right. It's just a job. If those idiots don't see the gem you are, good riddance."

"I—I got the j-j-job."

Teddy kept patting her back, rocking her back and forth. "Oh. Well, then. You don't want it?"

She shook her head. "I do. I *do* want it."

"You don't have to take it, Annabeth. You're a Boone now." He kept on rocking. "You can do anything you want. Hell, you could help me out here, at the Lodge. That'd be a real treat."

Her sobs kept coming.

"Aw, honey, you're breaking my heart." Teddy's voice was rough. "Been a long time since I comforted a woman. I'm afraid I'm not much good at it."

She shook her head as she pulled out of his arms. "You're the sweetest man, Teddy. I'm just an...emotional mess right now." She sniffed. "I'll take a shower."

"Ryder and I will get Cody to bed," Teddy offered.

"You don't have to—"

"Wouldn't have offered if I didn't want to." Teddy's voice was firm. "You go on, take a shower, read a book, whatever you need, you hear?"

Annabeth nodded, carrying the manila envelope into the bedroom with her. She closed the door, opened the envelope and scanned the information. They were giving her a raise—a big raise. No wonder Cutter was worked up. A big bump in medical benefits and retirement matching, as well. There was no way she could turn this down. She tossed the papers onto the bed, stripped and turned on the shower.

She rested her head against the tiles, willing the throb of her headache aside. She shampooed her hair, shaved her legs and stood under the jet until her skin was wrinkled. By the time she stepped out she was overheated and shaking. She didn't bother with her pajamas, or brushing her hair. She slipped into bed and stared up at the ceiling, her mind racing.

Her phone rang. It was Josie. "Hi."

"Annabeth? Do you have a cold?" Josie paused. "I'm so sorry I missed the meeting tonight. Eli had his Agriculture Club meeting and Hunter got called into the vet hospital for an emergency, so I was trying to be a good stepmom."

"Eli's meeting was probably more fun."

"Well?" Josie asked. "Are you still the principal of Stonewall Crossing?"

"I am." Annabeth tried for enthusiasm and ended up bursting into tears all over again.

"Annabeth?"

"I'm fine," she blubbered. "Just…so…emotional."

"I'm on my way."

"No, no," Annabeth pleaded. "I'm already in bed."

"It's seven forty-five." Josie sighed. "Please let me come over. I'll bring Eli. We can watch a chick flick and cry on your bed?"

She couldn't stop crying. "I'm already crying."

"Good." Josie laughed. "I'm on my way." She hung up before Annabeth could answer.

Annabeth tossed back the blankets, staring at her rounded stomach. Soon there would be no way to hide it. She wrapped her arms around the bump. "We're going to be okay," she whispered. "Your mom's got this single-mom thing down." Her own words set her off again. "I'll take care of you, I promise."

"Annabeth—" The anguish in Ryder's voice startled her.

She opened her mouth, but nothing came out. Why was he looking at her like that? Like he was hurting? She sniffed and wiped the tears from her face. "I'm tired." She bent to pull a nightie from the bedside drawer when her stomach clenched tightly. She covered her mouth and ran for the toilet, fighting her way into the nightie as she went.

Her stomach rejected the three licks of ice cream, half a sandwich and handful of crackers she'd eaten that day—as well as the extra-large protein smoothie she'd had for breakfast. She had nothing left, but her stomach kept heaving.

"This can't be normal." Ryder placed a cool washcloth against her forehead.

She shook her head, horrified that he was there. It was bad enough that she was an emotional wreck, but he was here, in the room, at her side, while she dry-heaved into the toilet. She held her hand up, croaking, "You don't have to be in here…"

He squatted beside her, rubbing the cool washcloth across her forehead again. "I need to be here," he argued. "I need to take care of you." His hand cradled her cheek, but she refused to meet his gaze. She was mortified. "Think you're done?" he asked.

She nodded slowly.

His strong hands clasped hers, pulling her up. Dizziness had her swaying where she stood, so Ryder swung her up into his arms. She didn't argue. She liked being in his arms, his big, warm, strong arms. She felt better there.

"You're skin and bones," he murmured.

"And babies," she added.

She could feel him smiling at her even though she refused to look at him as he placed her on the bed.

"Josie's coming over," Annabeth blurted out. "She heard me crying—"

"Why were you crying?" The anguish was back, forcing her to look at him.

He was so beautiful it hurt. "I… I'm pregnant."

He sat beside her on the bed, gently towel-drying her hair. His fingers brushed the nape of her neck. He set the towel down, sliding his fingers through the long locks of her hair. "Why are you so determined to keep me out?" His fingers kept moving, working gently through a snarl.

"I'm… I just…" Her mind raced. She'd made him a promise. She couldn't exactly say, *I love you and I want you to want to stay married to me even though I promised to divorce you once we knew about the job.* Could she?

She took a deep breath and forced herself to look at him. His brow was creased, his frown tense. As soon as he saw her gaze on him, he cocked an eyebrow at her. She touched the spot between his eyebrows, rubbing out the furrow there. He smiled, a lop-sided grin that had her heart pounding. His hand caught hers.

Maybe she should just spit it out there?

"Hey, guys." Josie arrived, carrying a bag. "I brought three tearjerkers, and two romantic comedies so we wouldn't get too maudlin."

Annabeth jumped up, then groaned.

"Come on, Princess." Ryder stood, leading her to the overstuffed chair in the corner. "You sit. I think Josie and I can get things set up."

"I don't think I ever want to get pregnant." Josie grimaced as she helped Ryder spread up the bed. "But I definitely want kids."

Ryder's expression was so comical, Annabeth had no choice but to laugh.

Ryder's pale blue eyes settled on her face and she was wrapped in the comfort of his smile. It would have been better if she'd never known how good it could be. If nothing else, her time with Ryder had reminded her that love was more than responsibilities and work—it was about joy and having fun. If he left tomorrow, she'd hold on to the memories they'd made together.

Chapter Fifteen

Ryder nudged his horse forward with a light squeeze of his knees. His father rode along the other side, clicking occasionally at the massive draft horse he preferred riding. Ryder smiled, enjoying the quiet companionability that had settled over them as they worked. He knew his father and knew he was up to something. He rarely rode fence lines anymore, but he'd volunteered to take Hunter's place that evening.

"Go ahead, Dad," Ryder prompted him.

Teddy tipped his beige hat back on his head and rested his hands on the horn of his saddle. "With what?"

Ryder sighed. "Speak your mind."

Teddy nodded. "Time was you'd have avoided riding out with me when you knew I had something to say."

Ryder couldn't argue. "Times change."

His words startled his father, but he nodded before saying, "You're working hard. And I appreciate it. Around here, with the ranch. At Annabeth's house—your house." His father turned all of his attention on him. "Is she expecting?"

"Yes, sir," Ryder said.

"Is that why you married her?"

Ryder nodded once.

"A lot of marriages start that way. Seen a few end because of it, too. I don't want that for you, son. I don't want that for any of you." Teddy shook his head. "She's a mighty stubborn little thing."

Which was an understatement. In the two weeks since the school board meeting, she'd spent every waking minute acting like he was a parent at her school. She was all professional charm, but she avoided any time alone with him—or eye contact. That didn't mean there was no hope. It just meant he had to try harder. Ryder laughed. "Yes, sir."

"But you love her. I can see it." Teddy clicked his tongue, keeping the horses moving along the barbed-wire fence as they talked. "Always have, if Renata's pictures are right." He looked at his son again. "She acts like you're leaving."

Ryder nodded.

"Is that the plan?" Ryder heard the tightness in his father's voice. "Are you leaving?"

"No, sir," he answered quickly. "But she seems to think so."

His father laughed. "Women are hard to work out. But your wife, well, I think I see where she's coming from. She was expecting when Greg passed on. She's expecting now and—with your history—I imagine she's waiting for you to go, too. Not die, but leave her alone." His father grinned. "It's what she knows, relying on herself."

Ryder stared at his father.

"Flo might have helped me figure some of this out," his father admitted. "I went to see her a few nights past and found her in her right mind. Not many women like Florence Chenault."

Ryder nodded, reeling from his father's newest revelation.

"Back in the day, we were close." His father laughed. "I figured she'd tell me what was going on, since you wouldn't."

His father's words stung.

"Not that you and I have ever been good at talking." His father held up a hand, adding, "That's my fault, not yours. But there comes a time when there's no way to avoid talking, so…"

Ryder cocked an eyebrow at his father. "So?"

"Start talkin'." His father glared at him. "How are you gonna keep Annabeth and Cody in the family?"

Ryder sat back in his saddle, looking up as the thin white clouds moved steadily across the sky. He wished he knew. "Guess I need to try harder." He'd sent flowers to her office, made ice cream runs, helped with the school field trip to the veterinary hospital and passed up two plum riding opportunities in case she needed anything. But all that seemed to do was irritate her even more.

"Have you tried talking?" his father asked.

Ryder grimaced. "We just said I'm no good at it."

"Who said that? I said we—" he pointed back and forth between the two of them "—weren't good at it. With other people? I'm not so sure."

"She's more likely to argue than listen," Ryder grumbled.

This time his father laughed. "Well, son, that's good news."

Ryder shot him a look. "How's that?"

"Arguing. Looks like that baby isn't the only thing you have in common."

Ryder shook his head. "Babies."

His father slapped his hand against his thigh. "I'll be." His father was all smiles for the rest of the ride.

But Ryder thought, maybe, his dad had a point. And, at this point, talking was the only thing he hadn't tried. He could only hope he'd find the right words.

ANNABETH STARED AT the flowers on her desk. Ryder had sent her yellow roses. Why? Because she loved yellow.

He'd also sent her lemon soda. Why? Because she liked lemons. It was like he was trying to lessen the blow that was coming. And it was coming, she knew it was. He'd been home late for the past few weeks, sneaking in when she was supposed to be sleeping. Even though all she'd done was lie there and worry. She had a hard time believing there were that many fences to mend or that there was a rodeo every night... Not that it mattered. It was good he was putting distance between them.

So all the little gifts were to ease his guilt. Did he think he could buy her off? That sneaking off to do whatever he was doing was okay? She'd hoped he'd behave until after they were divorced. And they hadn't even begun to talk about divorce proceedings.

Her attention wandered to the beautiful framed picture of her, Cody and Ryder at their wedding party. And another one, just the two of them. He was looking at her the way she was looking at him—as if there was love there.

She sighed, filing away the papers from this afternoon's parent-teacher conference and scrolling through her emails. She had a few parent complaints and a meeting request from the school board, but nothing too pressing. It could wait until tomorrow.

Right now, there was nothing she wanted more than to cook dinner with Cody and to try to hunt down her husband for a long-overdue talk. She loved him and she wanted him to know that. She didn't know if they could make it work, if he could find a way to love her forever, instead of for the time being.

She stopped by the gym for Cody, thanked Bryan for letting him hang out and drove Lady Blue to the Lodge.

"When's the h-house going to be fixed?" Cody asked.

"Ryder said there was so much work to be done that it was going to be a while. Tired of the Lodge?"

Cody laughed. "No way."

Annabeth shook her head. "Oh really?"

Cody nodded. She knew how close Teddy and Cody were getting, their love of model cars acting as a sturdy glue. But that's what worried her. Cody was getting too comfortable in the Boone family—they both were. Maybe the babies would ensure they were always family no matter what happened between her and Ryder. But how would she cope with that? Seeing what she wanted, what she had and what she lost.

She drew in a deep breath. No more speculating until she'd worked things out with Ryder.

"How about spaghetti and meatballs tonight?" she asked, turning at the impressive wrought-iron-and-stone gate that announced they'd reached Boone Ranch.

She saw Cody press his nose to the glass, hoping for a sighting of Uncle Hunter's whitetail or axis deer. Or maybe even some of the exotic game he'd started working with. Cody thought the animals were fascinating. Not as fascinating as cars, but a solid second. It probably helped that Eli was really into animals. He was older, the kind of kid someone Cody's age would look up to. The fact that he was a good kid, kind to Cody, respectful to his family, and funny, was a huge relief for Annabeth.

Teddy looked up from the check-in counter at the Lodge. "You're home early."

"I thought I'd make dinner for you tonight," she offered. "Spaghetti and meatballs? I know that's Ryder's favorite."

Teddy frowned. "He said something about working late tonight."

She nodded, trying not to be disappointed. "It'll keep."

Teddy's smile was strained. "I'm sure he'll be starved when he gets home."

"How was y-your day?" Cody asked Teddy, climbing up onto the stool beside the older man.

"Well, let's see. We have a couple here all the way from Minnesota. And a few businessmen thinking about renting the place out for a retreat or something. Other than that, it's been pretty quiet."

Cody nodded. "Had a s-spelling test."

Teddy nodded. "How'd it go?"

Cody shrugged. "D-dunno yet."

Annabeth smiled at the exchange. "Cody, why don't you go spend some time with Tom while I get started on dinner."

Cody nodded, hopping down and scurrying to his bedroom.

"You don't have to cook, Annabeth." Teddy was watching her. "There's stew and corn bread or chicken-fried steak in the dining room."

"For guests," she countered. "I appreciate it, Teddy, I do. But I have to do something to feel like I'm pulling my weight around here."

Teddy scratched his chin, then nodded. "I'm pretty partial to spaghetti and meatballs myself."

Annabeth smiled. "Good." In her room, she changed into some black leggings, one of the few things that didn't feel tight on her stomach. She tried on several T-shirts, but all of them hugged her bump in a way that left no doubt as to her condition. She gave up, pulling on one of Ryder's long flannel button-up shirts. She put her hair into a ponytail, slid on some slipper socks and headed back into the kitchen.

She was humming to the radio, rolling up meatballs, when she heard Ryder say hello to his father. She spun around as he entered the kitchen—looking dirty and tired and so handsome—it took everything she had not to welcome him home properly.

"You're not barefoot." His voice was low and gruff, a broad grin on his way-too-handsome face.

"It's a little too cold to be barefoot. And unsanitary—" Then she got it. Barefoot, pregnant and in the kitchen. She scowled at him. "Oh. I thought you were working late."

His smile faded. "Dad told me you were here."

She stopped, an uncooked meatball in her hand. "So you came home?"

"Nice shirt." He sat his tool belt on the bench and crossed the room. "We need to talk, Princess."

Her heart sank. "We do."

"I know what you're going to say." Ryder shoved his hands into his pockets. "So I want you to let me go first. Please."

"Okay." She forced the word out.

His frown deepened as his gaze traveled over every inch of her face. "I'm sorry I waited so long to do this." He sighed, opening then closing his mouth. His attention wandered to the meatball in her hand. "But I don't want to do this while I'm covered in dirt and sweat. Let me clean up first?"

She nodded, unable to speak. He was sorry. He was sorry he'd waited so long to end it? What was he sorry about? She turned back to her cooking, slapping the meatballs onto the tray and ignoring his exit from the room.

Cooking relaxed her. The meatballs went into the oven, and she started chopping onions, oregano, basil and mushrooms—stirring it into a hearty tomato sauce with a splash of red wine. She buttered the bread with her homemade garlic mixture and toasted it until it was crisp and light.

Cody helped her set the table. On the other side of the family kitchen, connected through the large pantry, was the industrial kitchen for the Lodge guests and special events. Annabeth had popped in there to borrow spices, overwhelmed by the fancy gadgets and high-end equipment the kitchen staff used. She made do with her four-burner gas cooktop and her oven just fine.

"Go tell Grandpa Teddy and Ryder dinner's ready." She dropped a kiss on Cody's head.

The phone rang but Annabeth ignored it, that's what Teddy had told her to do. The staff would pick it up, eventually. But it kept ringing, so she pulled a tablet and pen from the drawer and answered. "Boone Ranch, how can I help you?"

"Evening, this is Jerry Johannssen calling for Ryder Boone. He available?"

Annabeth didn't know the name. "He should be in for dinner any minute."

"Good, good—" Annabeth could hear another phone ringing on the other end of the line. "Hold on a sec." Jerry's voice was muffled. "I gotta take this call. Can you get a message to him for me?"

"Of course." She clicked the pen and waited.

"Just remind him I'm waiting for his phone call. I know he's got things to take care of there, but this is a once in a lifetime opportunity. Now I've got a pretty little 1969 Mustang just waiting for his touch. He can start tomorrow— all he needs to do is call me." He paused. "And that one-bedroom apartment is his, too."

She felt cold. "Apartment?" she murmured.

"Can't exactly commute to Dallas daily." Jerry laughed. "Just have him call me, will you?"

Annabeth stared at the words she'd written. *Ryder— Job in Dallas—One bedroom apartment—leaving tomorrow? Call Jerry Johannssen ASAP*. The black words were stark against the white page. "Yes. This job, this is a permanent position?"

"I sure as hell hope so." Jerry laughed. "Thank you kindly." And the phone went dead.

Annabeth set the phone on the marble counter. *We need to talk.* She was an idiot. A complete idiot. Of course he was making plans—she'd told him to. She'd let him know, every chance possible, that he was free to do whatever he wanted because she didn't need him.

She sat on the bench, her heart and stomach and head racing and churning and aching.

The way he looked at her tonight…it was goodbye.

Cody came bouncing back into the kitchen. "You o-okay?"

She pasted on a smile. "Great. Hungry."

"Me, too." Cody wrapped his arms around her neck and pressed a few kisses against her cheek. She hugged him to her, burying her face in his hair and taking comfort in his sweet scent.

"Something smells good." Renata swept into the kitchen.

"There's plenty." Annabeth put the heaping bowl of spaghetti down on top of the table. "How was your day?"

Renata shook her hand, dismissing it. "It's hard being a young person in an older community."

Teddy entered at that point. "Who's old?"

Renata smiled. "Not you, Dad, you get it. You understand you have to embrace new things, like technology, to advertise and draw new tourists."

"I'm hip," Teddy said, making everyone laugh.

"What did I miss?" Ryder asked, all wet hair and dashing smiles.

"Grandpa T-Teddy's f-funny," Cody said.

Annabeth placed the salad on the table and sat, trying not to react when Ryder sat beside her.

"Smells amazing," he said, serving himself a heaping helping.

"And it's your f-favorite," Cody added, nudging Annabeth with a smile.

She felt the heat in her cheeks, but refused to look at anything but the salad on her plate.

"Annabeth, that's not near enough food for you now," Teddy scolded. "Cody, get your ma a big glass of milk, too."

Cody hopped up.

Annabeth glanced at Ryder.

"Dad—" Ryder sighed.

"What? She needs to be eating more—a lot more." Teddy frowned, then went wide-eyed. "Oops."

Annabeth smiled. She couldn't help it.

Renata was staring at her, eyebrows arched and waiting.

Cody, oblivious, placed a huge glass of milk on the table. "Here you go."

Annabeth eyed the glass of milk. "That should do it."

"So?" Renata asked.

"Cody…" Annabeth took her son's hand. "I'm pregnant."

Renata jumped up, squealing, as she dropped a kiss on Ryder's cheek, then Annabeth's, then hugged Cody.

"What's that?" Cody asked.

"Your mom's giving you a brother or sister," Renata explained.

"Or one of each," Ryder added.

Annabeth didn't want to look at him. Not now. She wanted to enjoy this, to feel nothing but love and contentment. Instead, a hole was forming in her heart. And seeing the smile on Ryder's face was like salt to the world's worst paper cut. She tore her gaze from his and focused on Cody. This was big news for him and she didn't want him to be worried or upset.

"Twins?" Renata was squealing again, lifting Cody in her arms and spinning him around. "Two babies, Cody. What do you think of that?"

Cody giggled, wobbling on his feet when Renata sat him down.

"I'd say this deserves some celebrating." Teddy grabbed the phone. "I'm calling your brothers over for dinner."

"I'm not sure I made enough." Annabeth eyed the mountain of spaghetti.

But Teddy was heading out of the kitchen, talking to someone on the phone.

"There's enough for at least two weeks' worth of left-over lunches," Ryder said. He knew how frugal she was. He'd teased her about the stockpile of single-serving meals in her freezer. But she couldn't stand seeing anything go to waste.

"So, no leftovers," Renata agreed. "But plenty for the family." She pulled Annabeth to her feet and stood back to look at her. "Can I?"

Annabeth saw Renata's hand hovering over her stomach and nodded. "Sure. Nothing to feel yet—"

"Anytime now," Ryder interrupted.

He'd know. He spent more time reading the baby book than she did. Even though he knew the babies would be moving soon—that they were coming. Was he really planning on leaving?

Renata's hands pressed against her stomach, the soft fabric of Ryder's shirt rubbing against her skin. "That's quite a bump." It was easy to see Renata was figuring out when things had happened. When she stood up, she looked back and forth between Ryder and Annabeth curiously.

Cody came forward, pulling up her shirt to stare at her stomach. "Hi," he said. "And hi."

Annabeth felt the sting of tears in her eyes and ruffled her son's fine blond hair.

Ryder's hand was warm against the skin on her back. "I'm sure they're saying hi right back, Cody." He knelt beside the boy.

Cody was staring intently at the swell of her stomach. "Does it hurt?"

Annabeth laughed, watching her son. "No."

"Be sweet to Mom," Cody spoke softly. "She's the best. Don't worry about n-nothing. R-Ryder and I can p-protect you. And Tom will, too."

Ryder was looking at her, she could tell. She shouldn't look at him, but she did. She could spend hours lost in those eyes, pretending he loved her the way she craved. It would be easy to reach out and slide her fingers through the short dark blond hair, stroke the side of his face. Her hand itched to do it. She flexed her fingers, fighting the instinct.

Ryder captured her hand and pressed a kiss to her palm. It was impossible to resist touching him then. Her fingers rested along his cheek, absorbing his warmth.

Chapter Sixteen

It took less than fifteen minutes for all the Boones to converge. More chairs were added, making it close quarters. She was almost in Ryder's lap when everyone was seated, but she tried not to think about it. Instead, she watched the dynamics of the family around her.

The brothers were fascinating, every conversation lined with a competitive yet playful edge. Other than Teddy, Hunter seemed the most content. The love he and Josie shared was evident in every glance and touch. She'd never know Eli was Josie's stepson, the bond there was so strong and real. A lot like watching Ryder and Cody... Her chest ached.

Archer was the most aloof, observing everyone without any obvious reaction. He didn't smile often or have much to say about anything but work. But when he caught her eye, he raised his glass in a quick salute. She smiled, nodding in return.

Fisher kept people laughing. He knew how to make everyone welcome and entertained. Especially the boys. Eli and Cody were in stitches as Fisher shared a story about one of the fourth-years at the veterinary hospital and a very affectionate Great Dane.

She was smiling, too, caught up in the boys' laughter, when Ryder shifted. His hand rested on her thigh. And, try as she might, she was instantly aware of his breath on her shoulder, the low rumble of his laughter.

She all but jumped up to clear the table when the food was gone.

"That was delicious." Fisher smiled down at her. "Thanks for the eats, sis," he added, winking.

"Glad you enjoyed it."

"You headed over later?" Fisher asked Ryder so softly she wasn't sure she'd heard correctly.

But Ryder led him out of the room and she was left with Renata and Josie and cleanup duty.

"You should sit and actually eat something." Renata shook her head. "You didn't eat anything except a carrot stick. And you didn't touch the milk Cody got you."

She smiled, scrubbing the garlic from the pan. "I'm fine."

"I bet there's some Italian crème cake left in the other kitchen," Renata kept going. "No one can say no to Bitty's cake."

"I'm fine—"

"Renata's gone." Josie laughed. "She's right, Annabeth. You're eating for three. Three." Josie paused, eyeing Annabeth's stomach. "Eat some cake and don't feel guilty about it."

Renata carried a cake plate back into the kitchen as they finished the dishes. "Y'all sit, and I'll get plates. How's the new book going, Josie?"

Josie was a children's author and illustrator. Her books were about a little country town a lot like Stonewall Crossing. And, to Annabeth, her friend's illustrations were worthy of framing.

"Things are good. Nothing like finding your rhythm." Josie took a bite of cake and closed her eyes. "This is too good."

Annabeth shrugged and took a bite. Good was a huge understatement.

Renata chattered on about her work at the tourism department for the county. Annabeth listened. She had to get through tonight, finalize everything with Ryder, before she could deal with anything else. Would she still be welcome for cake and chit-chat once she was the former Mrs. Ryder Boone? Her stomach clenched and she dropped her fork.

"You okay?" Renata asked.

"Fine." She tried to smile, but the clenching didn't ease.

"Annabeth, you look really pale." Josie took her hand. "You sure you're okay?"

"I'm fine." Annabeth stood. "I'm going to check on Cody." She hoped being on her feet, stretching, might ease the cramps. Cody and Eli lay on the floor of the great room, a game of checkers underway. She waved and decided a walk and fresh air would do her some good. She slipped out the back door and onto the wide wraparound porch. She moved slowly, resting against the support beams now and then, and thinking calm thoughts. She had to relax—all this stress wasn't good for the babies.

She walked all the way around the house and found Ryder on the front porch, talking on the phone.

"I already told you I can't make it tonight." Ryder laughed. "Maybe tomorrow."

She leaned against the railing.

"I have a few things to work out here…" He laughed again. "She doesn't know. Not yet."

Doesn't know what? Was he talking to Mr. Johannssen? Was this about his new job? His new life? She was sitting with his family, eating cake, talking about their babies and the future, and he was…already moving on. Talking to her was the only thing holding him back. Maybe she should approach the situation like a Band-Aid. It would hurt less ripping it off quickly.

"Ryder?"

He turned, his smile disappearing. "Gotta go."

"We can't keep putting off our talk." She wrapped her arms around herself. "I know you said you wanted to go first, but I can't wait."

He frowned, looking around them. He stepped closer to her, but she stopped him.

"I need you to know how much I appreciate everything you've done for me and Cody. Because I do. But it's time for me and Cody to go home." She refused to look at him, it hurt too much. "Our home."

"Annabeth…" His hands settled on her shoulders. "Come on—"

She shook her head. "I'm done. I can't do this anymore. I know I'm emotional and pregnant, but I'm not the only one that's involved here. We're going to hurt so many people. Cody?" She shook her head. "It's not fair to him, don't you see? I have the job, there's no reason for you to stay with us." Her voice was shaking.

"No reason?" he hissed, his hold tightening.

She stared at him, her words so thick they almost choked her. "They will always be your children. I'll never keep them from you. But I can't keep pretending that you want anything else from me, Ryder. That you want me when this was never about you and me. My heart can't take it anymore, don't you understand that? This won't last. We both know it. I've got to get over you so I can learn to be on my own again. We've made such a horrible mistake, don't you see that?" She shrugged out of his hold. "So, please, please, just go."

He stood there, staring at her.

"I know you have other plans…that you're moving on.

There's a one bedroom-apartment and a job waiting for you in Dallas right now. It's time to live your life—the life you *want*." She shook her head. "If we could leave the Lodge, we would, but Cody and I are stuck right now. Please." She swallowed. "It would be best for me... Please, stay in your apartment."

His eyes bore into hers, intense and searching. "This is really what you want? Me...gone?"

No. She wanted him to argue, to tell her he loved her. "It's what I need," she murmured.

She didn't watch him walk down the steps of the porch or drive his truck away. She sat, blindly, in one of the rocking chairs on the porch of the Lodge. By the time the sun disappeared on the horizon, Annabeth knew something was wrong.

RYDER SLAMMED HIS sledgehammer into the cracking plaster, gratified when the whole wall came free and collapsed.

Annabeth's words spun in his head until it ached. She needed him to leave. She needed him to leave her alone.

He made short work of the wall, venting his frustration on the warped wood and rusted nails.

He knew he hadn't done enough, but he'd held on to hope that she'd see what they could be. That she'd find a way to believe in him. To see what he wanted to be. He'd hoped that would be enough.

His phone rang.

"Drinkin' tonight?" DB asked.

Ryder was breathing hard, dripping sweat and exhausted.

"Or you still too tangled up in her skirts to think for yourself?" DB prodded.

"No," he bit out. No matter how much he wanted to be tangled up in those skirts.

"I'll come get you," DB offered.

Ryder wiped his face on a towel, then hung it back on one of the newly framed walls. "I'll meet you there." He hung up, staring at the phone in his hand. He didn't have to ask where they were going, it was always the same place. Same drinks, different women.

He drew in a deep breath, but it didn't help the pain in his chest.

My heart can't take it anymore...

All he wanted to do was take care of her heart, body— all of her. He didn't want to hurt her. And it killed him that she didn't see that.

His phone rang again. He groaned when he saw his brother's number. "Leave me alone," he ground out.

"No, I sure as hell won't," Hunter bit back. "Where are you?"

"I don't need your shit right now, Hunter—"

Hunter cut him off. "Annabeth's in the hospital, Ryder."

Ryder was running out the door before he knew where he was going. His heart was racing, pure unfiltered terror clawing his insides. He jumped into the truck, started the engine and peeled out, stomping on the gas and flying down the street to the highway.

He left the truck in the emergency driveway and ran inside, fear driving him. His father was there. So were Josie and Hunter.

Josie pointed. "She's in the back."

Ryder headed in that direction, ignoring his brother's scowl and his father's concern. Right now, they didn't matter. He just needed to know she was okay.

"Sir," a nurse was calling out to him, but he ignored her, peeking behind curtains as he went. "Sir!"

He froze, turning to glare at her. "My wife. Annabeth Boone?"

The woman glared right back. "Follow me."

He wanted to scream at her to tell him where Annabeth was so he could get there faster. She was alone—

"In here," the woman said. "Calm. You hear me? She doesn't need any excitement."

He brushed past the woman into the dimly lit room. Annabeth lay on her left side, her hands resting on her stomach. She had a belt around her belly and the room was filled with a strange alternating, static-sounding beat. She looked so still, thin and fragile. As though he could break her by touching her.

He crossed the room and bent low, pressing kisses along her brow. "Annabeth?"

She turned, her eyes fluttering open. "Ryder?" Her chin crumpled.

"I'm here, Princess." He sat on the bed, resting his forehead against hers. "Just let me stay."

Tears spilled from her beautiful hazel eyes and down her cheeks.

"I love you, Annabeth. I love you." His hands tangled in her hair. "Don't ask me to leave you, because I can't. Whether or not you think you need me, I know I need you. I can't lose you."

She was crying, hard sobs racking her body.

"Shh." He held her close, his eyes burning. "What do you need? Tell me, whatever it is—let me do something."

She slipped her arms around his neck. "Stay."

He relaxed, melting against her. He was on the verge of tears, but he had to be strong. Together, they could handle whatever was happening. As long as he had her, it would be okay. He kissed her, cupping her cheeks, rubbing her tears away. "What did the doctor say? What happened?"

"I stood up—" she sniffed "—and got so dizzy. I guess I fainted."

He frowned, kissing her forehead, then her cheeks. He didn't want to think about her lying on the ground. "Why'd you do something like that?" he tried to tease.

She laughed, stroking his face with her hand. He covered her hand with his, pressing a kiss to her palm.

"I wasn't there to catch you," he murmured, his voice gruff.

"I'm sorry, Ryder—"

"Shh, we'll figure this out." He kissed her again. "You know why I call you Princess, Annabeth?" She shook her head. "That's how I see you. Like a princess from a bedtime story. Sweet, giving, smart and funny. A good woman. Beautiful in every way." He smoothed her hair back again. "Better than anything I'll ever deserve. But everything I've always wanted. Calling you Princess helps me remember how special you are. And how damn lucky I am."

She was staring at him with round, damp eyes.

"It's going to be okay. Doc Meyer will know what's wrong—"

"Probably looking at pre-eclampsia," a voice from behind them announced.

Ryder barely moved. "Doc Meyer," he said.

"Ryder." Doc Meyer checked the monitor, flipped through Annabeth's chart, then sighed. "How are you feeling Annabeth?"

"Tired," she answered.

"I need to examine her, Ryder, so you'll have to move." Doc Meyer put his hands on his hips.

Ryder stood, but didn't let go of Annabeth's hand—no way anyone would make him let go of her.

Doc Meyer sighed again, but there was a small smile on his face. "We're going to check on the twins. Heartbeat sounds good."

Ryder realized that was what the static thumping was and smiled down at Annabeth. She looked so scared it tore his heart out. He crouched on the floor at her head, smoothed her hair back and kissed her forehead. "Everything's gonna be okay. You hear me?"

She nodded once, her gaze locking with his. "I hear you."

A nurse wheeled a cart into the room. He ignored everything but Annabeth, smoothing her hair, twining his fingers through hers, smiling at her. He hated feeling helpless.

"There we go." Doc Meyer was pointing at the screen on the cart. "Looks like we have a boy...yes... A healthy boy, from the looks of him."

Ryder stared at the screen, smiling at the image that greeted him. His son.

The screen went black, then another baby.

"And a daughter. One of each. She's a tiny thing...but... she looks good, too..." Doc Meyer kept clicking buttons. "I'd say we're pushing twenty-four weeks. Too early to deliver."

Ryder had never felt such excitement and concern all at once. "And Annabeth?"

"Well..." Dr. Meyer looked over her chart again. "Could be pre-eclampsia. Could be diet or stress. Her BP was a little high when she came in, but it's fine now. We'll need to run a few tests to see for sure."

"If it's pre-eclampsia?" Annabeth's voice was soft.

"Bed rest. Here or at home." Doc Meyer looked at the two of them.

"Home, please," Annabeth asked.

"Whatever Doc Meyer says, Princess." He shook his head. "I'm not taking any chances with you."

Doc Meyer cocked an eyebrow. "Let's see what the

tests say. We'll need to get some blood. Annabeth, Nurse Garcia will help you to the restroom for a urine sample."

"I'll help," he offered.

"They're not going far, Ryder." Doc Meyer peered at him over the rim of his glasses. "We'll both be in earshot."

He didn't care what Doc Meyer said. He watched the nurse unhook Annabeth from several devices, help her into the wheelchair, then to the bathroom.

"You okay?" Doc Meyer asked Ryder.

Ryder closed his eyes, the enormity of the situation hitting him. "Just tell me what I have to do to keep her safe, Doc. Then I'll be okay."

Chapter Seventeen

Annabeth strolled down the stone patch and over the hill to the dock. She paused, soaking up the heat of the afternoon sun and the pure contentment she felt at the sight that greeted her. Ryder and Cody, side by side in straw cowboy hats and plaid shirts, each holding a fishing pole. Beside them sat two pairs of boots, Ryder's tackle box and the picnic basket she brought to them hours before. She smiled, the sounds of their conversation growing louder the closer she got.

Seeing Ryder with Cody filled her with contentment. She had a family now, people who would always be there for her and Cody. All thanks to her husband. And tonight she would tell Ryder how much she loved him. She'd spent so much time being scared—finding excuses not to tell him the truth even after she *knew* he loved her. But she wasn't afraid anymore. She loved him. She needed him. And she was thankful he was her husband. He should know that.

"Bigger the grasshopper, the bigger the fish," Ryder was saying.

"And they aren't slimy like worms," Cody added, enunciating clearly.

"Never was much for worms," Ryder agreed.

"Except for the ones you'd chase the girls around the playground with?" she asked.

They both looked up at her, wearing almost identical grins. Her heart thumped. She was one lucky woman.

"Well, now, that's an entirely different use. A better use for a worm, if you ask me." Ryder winked at her. "Remember that, Cody."

She rolled her eyes. "Cody, Grandpa Teddy said your show was coming on?"

Cody and Teddy had taken to watching some car-restoration program together. Annabeth had tried to sit through it a few times, but ended up dozing off.

Cody nodded, reeling in his line. "Thanks, Ma." He put his things away, pulled on his boots, gave her a quick hug and ran back to the Lodge.

"He's going to hate moving back to the house." Annabeth watched Cody go. There was room here, to run and play and be a boy.

Ryder packed his things up, glancing up at her. "He'll be fine." Ryder stood, stretching. He held out his hand to her. "Come here."

She hugged him, smiling up at him. "Catch anything?"

"Just you." He kissed her, laughing when an especially hard kick from the twins hit him in the stomach. "They're feisty tonight." He bent, speaking to her stomach. "You two go easy on your mom." He grinned up at her. "Up for going out?"

She nodded. Nervous, but excited, too. "Getting a little stir-crazy. And Doc Meyer said I was fine. Clear for normal activities." She pulled him up. "Are you trying to break our date?"

"No, ma'am." Ryder stared down at her. "A whole night with my wife to myself? Not a chance."

"Renata's here, with pizza. Your dad found some car show marathon—poor Renata. And the bags are in the truck." She took the hand he offered, following him back up the trail to the Lodge. "Still won't tell me where we're going?" She sighed when he shook his head. "Is it far?" The bigger she got, the harder it was to sit still for long periods of time.

"Not far." He opened the back door into the Lodge.

She felt great, reenergized, more than ready to go back to work in a week. And very enthusiastic about a night with her husband. Ryder was still being extracareful with her, a little too careful with her. But she had high hopes for tonight.

Things had changed since that awful night in the hospital. Most importantly, Ryder loved her. He told her, regularly. And when he didn't say it, he showed it in a way that left no room for doubt.

And, she'd taken the job—then immediately gone on a three-week leave of absence. Ken was all too happy to step in while she was getting the rest Doc Meyer said she needed. Rest and food. Her test results proved she was dehydrated and anemic, and several pounds underweight. Ryder, Cody and Teddy were relentless in their devotion to "fattening her up."

She pressed a kiss to Cody's forehead, thanked Teddy and hugged Renata before Ryder pulled her out the front door and into his truck.

"You in a hurry?" she asked.

"It's getting late. We're losing daylight," he said, as if that explained anything.

"And daylight is necessary for…?" she teased, taking a moment to appreciate her husband's strong profile.

He laughed. "You'll see."

Ryder drove into town, past the elementary school and toward her house. But instead of turning right, he turned left…and stopped in front of the Czinkovic place. The for-sale sign was gone and Ryder's motorcycle was parked out front.

Annabeth stared out the window, frozen.

She was looking at Cody's picture. From the fresh lilac-blue paint with bright white trim and detailed work to the shining stained-glass windows at the top of the gable. The porches, which had drooped sadly, were straight and level. Even the yard had been overhauled, blooming with yellow lantana, tulips and irises waving happily in the spring breeze.

She stepped out of the car, shock and joy leaving her speechless.

In the backyard, in the perfect tree-house tree, was Cody's tree house. It had the winding staircase with a rope bannister and an elevator for Tom—just like his picture. She pressed a hand to her mouth, torn between laughing and sobbing. She couldn't stop the tears that rolled down her cheek, or the joy that washed over her.

Several thumps from her belly and she looked down, running her hands over her belly. "You two are so lucky. You have the best daddy in the world."

RYDER CLIMBED OUT of the truck, watching her with a full heart. The look on her face made every early morning and late night working worth it. He smiled as she said something to her stomach, her hands smoothing her yellow shirt into place. She walked to the tree house, her long hair and white skirts blowing in the breeze, as she circled the base of the tree. He followed her, equal parts excitement and anxiety. Trying to give the woman he loved her childhood dream was no small thing.

"You're amazing." Her voice shook, heavy with emotion. "It's too much."

"No, it's not." He brushed the hair from her shoulder.

She stepped forward, wrapping her arms around his waist. The swell of her belly brought out a fierce protectiveness in him. And a sense of peace he'd never felt before. That night, seeing her in that hospital bed, put everything into perspective. Annabeth and Cody were all that mattered—and the twins. No matter what, if he had them life was pretty damn good.

Her voice was muffled against his chest. "Cody is going to be thrilled."

"I hope so. He's gotten pretty attached to Dad." Ryder breathed deep, drawing her scent in. "As much as I'd like to take all the credit, it was a family project. And my brothers had their own opinion on a lot of things. My dad, too." But working toward this, building their family, had brought him closer to his dad than ever before. "Hope we got it right."

"Are you kidding?" She looked up at him. "It's perfect, Ryder."

He grinned. He'd be content to stay just like this, holding her close. But there was more to show her. "We're not done yet. Come on." He let her go, then took her hand in his.

Each room had been completely redone. He'd refinished the floors, repaired the wiring, removed a few walls to open the place up and repainted every square inch. Once that was done, he'd brought over whatever furniture they could salvage from her house. He'd added a few new additions, like the china hutch that displayed her grandmother's china.

"Made sure all the doors are handicap-accessible, too," he murmured, watching the sheer amazement on her lovely face. "For Flo's Sunday dinners. I figure we could rotate between here and the Lodge so Dad's included."

"Ryder…" She walked through the house, opening and closing cabinets and doors. He showed her downstairs, the things he'd pulled from Flo's storage unit, her house and contributions from his family, too. It was truly their home.

He showed her the bed he and John had built for Cody from car parts. "It's safe, no sharp edges, promise." He ran his hand along the steering wheel. "Thought he'd get a kick out of it."

"This is amazing. He will… He will flip." She shook her head.

He led her down the hall to the babies' room, pushing open the door. He'd asked Josie for help and his sister-in-law had delivered. The walls were covered in a gorgeous mural of fairy-tale castles and nursery-rhyme characters.

"A princess." She glanced at one of the details.

He smiled broadly. "Of course."

"So this must be you?" She pointed at the knight on a white horse.

Ryder shook his head. "Dad wanted you to know he made sure we followed the crib instructions. He hovered every second, double-checking our work. I thought Archer was going to pop a gasket."

Annabeth was sniffing when she faced him. "Ryder, how…? When…?"

"Every spare second." He shrugged.

"But…" She shook her head, looking around the nursery. "It's so much work."

"I don't mind working." He grinned. "I think we all enjoyed it."

"It's too much."

"Not for you, Princess."

She shook her head, her gaze traveling slowly over his

face. "Since the night you proposed, you've done nothing but take care of me and Cody." She paused. "No, since before that."

He cupped her cheek, staring into her huge hazel eyes. "I've loved you a long time, Annabeth."

Her eyes closed briefly. "I'm sorry." She paused and his heart seemed to stop. "I'm so sorry I haven't shown you the same love and respect you give me, every day." She swallowed, covering his hand with hers. "But I'll spend the next thirty or so years trying to make up for it, I promise." A tear slipped from the corner of her eye. "It scares me how much I love you, Ryder Boone."

His heart thudded against his chest, filling his body with real happiness. He'd wanted that for so long, but never dared to hope. Hope was a dangerous thing.

"But what scares me more is you not knowing that. I guess I was scared that telling you would change things. That it would scare you…or something. But now I know better. I trust you. I trust us." She paused. "And I'm so glad you're their father." She put his hand on her stomach. "And Cody's father." She stood on tiptoe, twining her arms around his neck. His arms slid around her back. "I packed Option A. You'd mentioned burning it? Or shredding it. Your call. It's not what I want." Her gaze held his. "I know I can make it on my own. But, for the first time in my life, I don't want to. I *need* you." Her voice wavered. "I don't have any way to show you what you mean to me, Ryder…nothing that compares to this." She gestured to the house with one hand, holding on to his with the other.

He rested his forehead against hers, her words filling all the empty spaces in his heart. She needed him. She wanted him. She loved him. He had everything he'd always wanted. "Say it again," he murmured, stooping to kiss her full lips.

"I love you," she whispered, her hands cradling his face as she pressed kisses along his cheek and nose. "I love you."

"I'd say that's a mighty good place to start, Princess."

* * * * *

REQUEST YOUR FREE BOOKS!
2 FREE NOVELS PLUS 2 FREE GIFTS!

HARLEQUIN®

American Romance®

LOVE, HOME & HAPPINESS

A soft, concerned and decidedly male voice interrupted
her from just outside the corral.

"Are you all right?"

She quickly gathered herself, using the sleeve of
her denim jacket to wipe her face. "I'm fine," she said,
sounding stronger than she felt.

"You sure?"

She dared a peek over the top of Hurry Up's mane, only
to quickly duck down.

Josh Dempsey, August's oldest son, stood watching
her. She recognized his brown Resistol cowboy hat and
tan canvas duster through the sucker rod railing. Of all the
people to find her, why him?

Heat raced up her neck and engulfed her face. Not from
embarrassment, but anger. It wasn't that she didn't like
Josh. Okay, to be honest, she didn't like him. He'd made
it clear from the moment he'd arrived at Dos Estrellas a
few months ago that he wanted the land belonging to the
mustang sanctuary.

She understood. To a degree. The cattle operation
was the sole source of income for the ranch, and the
sanctuary—operating mostly on donations—occupied a
significant amount of valuable pastureland. In addition,

Cara didn't technically own the land. She'd simply been granted use of the two sections and the right to reside in the ranch house for as long as she wanted or for as long as the ranch remained in the family.

Sympathy for the struggling cattle operation didn't change her feelings. She needed the sanctuary. She and the two-hundred-plus horses that would otherwise be homeless. For those reasons, she refused to concede, causing friction in the family.

Additional friction. Gabe Dempsey and his half brothers, Josh and Cole, were frequently at odds over the ranch, the terms of their late father's will and the mustang sanctuary.

"You need some help?" Josh asked from the other side of the corral.

"No."

"Okay."

But he didn't leave.

Without having to glance up, she felt his height and the breadth of his wide shoulders. He looked at her with those piercing blue eyes of his.

She'd seen his eyes flash with anger—at his brother Gabe and at her for having the audacity to stand up to him. She'd also seen them soften when he talked about his two children.

"I'm sorry," he said with a tenderness in his voice that she'd never heard before. "Violet told me earlier. About your son."

*Don't miss COME HOME, COWBOY by Cathy McDavid, part of the **MUSTANG VALLEY** miniseries, available February 2016 wherever Harlequin® American Romance® books and ebooks are sold.*

www.Harlequin.com

Love the Harlequin book you just read?

Your opinion matters.

Review this book on your favorite book site, review site, blog or your own social media properties and share your opinion with other readers!

Be sure to connect with us at:
Harlequin.com/Newsletters
Facebook.com/HarlequinBooks
Twitter.com/HarlequinBooks

THE WORLD IS BETTER WITH

Romance

Harlequin has everything from contemporary, passionate and heartwarming to suspenseful and inspirational stories.

Whatever your mood,
we have a romance just for you!

Connect with us to find your next great read, special offers and more.